Martin, Nora.
The eagle's shadow

DATE DUE			

The Eagle's Shadow

Nora Martin

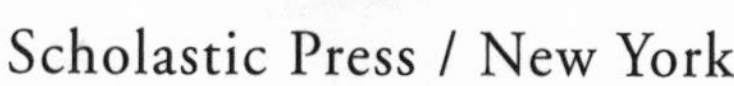

Scholastic Press / New York

 Published by Scholastic Press, a division of Scholastic Inc.,
Publishers since 1920. SCHOLASTIC and SCHOLASTIC PRESS and associated logos
are trademarks and/or registered trademarks of Scholastic Inc.

Library of Congress Cataloging-in-Publication Data
Martin, Nora.
The Eagle's shadow / by Nora Martin.
p. cm.
Summary: In 1946, while her emotionally distant father is in occupied Japan, a twelve-year-old girl spends a year with her mother's relatives in a Tlingit Indian village in Alaska and begins to love and respect her heritage as she confronts the secret of her mother's disappearance.
ISBN 0-590-36087-6 (hc)
1. Tlingit Indians — Juvenile fiction. [1. Tlingit Indians — Fiction. 2. Indians of North America — Alaska — Fiction. 3. Alaska — Fiction. 4. Alcoholism — Fiction.] I. Title.
PZ7.M364155Eag 1997 [Fic] — dc21 96-29902

10 9 8 7 6 5 4 3 2 1

Printed in the U.S.A.
First edition, September 1997
Design by David Caplan

For my husband,
Andrew Hansen, who showed me eagles

1
BIG MOON
DIS ATL-AN

A year ago my world was water. I felt as if I were drowning in it with nothing solid to grab. I stood on the bow of a small mail boat as it traveled northwestward over choppy waves. Surrounding me were clouds so heavy with gray rain that their fat bellies skimmed the water. And like the wet mists that pressed in on my skin, my life swirled in confusion. I couldn't turn around, but I was afraid to go on.

It's now been almost a year since that day I came to Alaska with nothing but my aloneness. Then, I was like my mother and father. I didn't know about families. I didn't know that wool and wood and eagles were all my family as much as the people in my house. I didn't know Mark, Grandma Martha, Aunt Ivy, and Uncle Samuel.

And I didn't know that, because of me, Henry Jonee would be sent to jail.

It was in August of nineteen forty-six, in our apartment on the army base in Tacoma, Washington, that my father told me he was being assigned overseas to occupied Japan.

"Clearie, I'm sending you to your grandmother in Alaska while I'm gone. You can stay with her."

"I've never even met her," I said. "Why can't I go with you?"

"I'll be gone for at least a year," he said. He looked at me, but then moved his stare to the wall just behind my head. "Besides, my duties in Japan won't leave me time for —" he paused — "for family. You're twelve years old, for crying out loud. Certainly you can start taking care of yourself."

My father's hand turned tense white where he gripped his knee. He wasn't a large man. Sitting beside him I looked almost straight into his eyes.

"You're a big girl," he said.

Yes, too big to pretend I don't exist, I thought to myself. I would never be brave enough to say it out loud.

Father put me on the boat in Tacoma two months later. "I'll write," he said. I couldn't stop my tears and my hands shook where they gripped the rail.

I tried to photograph him in my mind, with his blue eyes and light sandy hair, but he headed to the car before the boat even left.

After eight days I arrived in Juneau, where I boarded a local mail boat for the last forty-eight hours of my trip. From the deck of the mail packet I saw the tiny dock surrounded by wooden houses that was my destination. A dozen fishing boats clustered in the bay. Everywhere else tree-frosted hillsides flowed, like waterfalls, down to the water's edge.

On the dock, my grandmother waited for me. Grandma Martha is my mother's mother. Dora, my mother, was born and raised in this Tlingit Indian village.

I barely remembered my mother, and I knew nothing of this place she came from. When I asked my father about Tahkeen he only said, "It rains a lot." When I asked about my mother he became angry and said, "What's to know? She's gone."

The boat bumped easily against the dock that jutted out from the shore on thick stilts. Three people huddled under raincoats and flat-brimmed rubber hats. Their shadowed faces and green rain clothes made them look exactly like this rain-soaked place, like camouflage. I was the only passenger, and they came to greet me.

The woman in the center was short and round. The rubber coat she wore hung around her ankles. She looked out from under the dripping hat. I knew this must be my grandmother.

"Welcome, Granddaughter," she said. She held my face in her large cold hands and studied my hazel eyes and bark-brown hair. I saw her shake her head as she noticed my wet clothes. "We must hurry you home."

My grandmother looked just like I remembered my mother when I was very young. She had the same wide round face with hair low on her forehead. But Grandma Martha's face was lined and dark.

Finally, the younger woman stepped forward. "Hello, Clearice. I'm your Aunt Ivy," she said. "This is Samuel, your great-uncle."

"He is my brother," Grandma Martha said warmly.

I was surprised. My father never mentioned any relatives other than Grandma Martha. He just said many of the people in the village were related in one way or another. Uncle Samuel was small. His face looked like a weathered piece of wood, but his eyes were like shiny black stones. Uncle Samuel nodded at me but didn't say anything.

Aunt Ivy was taller than Grandma Martha. When she leaned toward me, I saw her hair hung in a thick braid down her back.

"Come," Aunt Ivy said. "Uncle Samuel will get your things." He pushed a wheelbarrow past us to the boat.

Aunt Ivy put a hand on my shoulder and steered me up the dock toward the clutter of buildings. We turned and walked on an uneven wooden sidewalk.

"You look like your mother," Grandma Martha said. "Except your hair is lighter than Dora's was and there is some curl in it. And Ivy, she is tall like Dora and you."

"Let's hope she is more pleasant than Dora," Aunt Ivy said.

I saw Grandma Martha shake her head at Ivy. I couldn't think of what to say. I still felt like I did on the boat, as if I was watching everything through a thick fog. Why would Aunt Ivy talk about my mother that way? When she touched my hair, I moved away.

It was almost dark, but I could see two rows of houses set along a muddy road. The houses by the water were built on pilings like the dock. The high tide slipped quietly underneath them. The other row sat against a wall of dark forest. Some of the windows in the houses glowed a soft yellow. I could hear an engine running in the distance behind me. The heavy rain pulled the wood smoke down to the ground. My nose tingled with the musky smells of smoke, wet wood, and salt water.

While we walked, Grandma Martha asked me questions about my trip. Her voice seemed to stop after each word like tiny separate sentences, whereas my voice flowed out in a solid stream, fast and hard. I wondered if everyone here sounded like that, the way I dimly remembered my mother speaking.

Aunt Ivy stopped in front of a small weathered house on the water side of the street. In the darkness, the white porcelain door handle glowed like a full moon. I was cold. The rain seeped through my clothes.

Inside, Grandma held a match to a gaslight on the wall. Then she lit a kerosene lamp on the table. We stood under a low ceiling where a huge wood cookstove took up one corner of the room. Behind the table, a smaller barrel stove radiated warmth. In one wall a stairway led upstairs, and another door closed off a room toward the water. I could hear waves lap the beach through the floorboards beneath my feet.

"I'll boil tea," Grandma Martha said. She pumped water at the sink into an aluminum teakettle.

On the dim walls hung pieces of carved wood and a large triangular blanket. There was a shiny new bolt lock on the door.

I looked at the flickering lamp on the table. "Why don't you have electricity?"

"There is no electricity to have," Grandma Martha said. "This isn't a city like Juneau."

"The church and Tom Jonee at the store have gasoline generators," Aunt Ivy said. That must have been the engine sound I heard while walking up from the boat.

"What about radio?" I asked. I couldn't believe they wouldn't at least have that.

The three of them just shook their heads. "No radio," Grandma Martha said.

"What do you do in the evening?" The thought of long hours with nothing to listen to seemed impossible.

"Do?" Grandma Martha looked completely confused.

"You know," I said. "For fun and entertainment."

"Sometimes we take a walk," Grandma Martha's face looked hopeful.

Aunt Ivy opened a door. "Here is your room." She walked ahead of me with the lamp held high to light the way. The narrow room hung over the water. With shelves lining the wall by the door, it looked as if it had been a closet or pantry. One step over, a narrow bed and crate-box table sat under a window that looked out to the blackness of the bay. The room was freezing. I sat down on the bed and tried to see through the window, but the only things visible were raindrops clinging to the outside of the glass.

Uncle Samuel came in with my boxes and suitcase.

Aunt Ivy said, "Put some dry clothes on. Then come eat."

When I came out into the main room, Aunt Ivy was putting plates of fish on the table. On each plate there was a square piece of pale pink fish with tiny bits of white fat on it and two round biscuits sitting next to the fish. Aunt Ivy set a bowl of gravy on the table in front of me. The smell was strong.

"It's salmon," Grandma Martha said. "Good stuff."

I poked at it with my fork.

"Your eyes are so light," Grandma Martha said, staring at me. "But your face is strong and round; that is from your mother and from me."

"Clearice," Aunt Ivy said. "Do you hear from Dora?"

I had known they would ask about my mother, but it was still hard to answer. "No, we never heard anything from her," I said. "I was only five when she left. I hardly remember her."

"Dora never wrote to us," Aunt Ivy said. "She was always angry. Angry and hateful."

"She was born with a *lekwaa x'ann* inside her," Grandma Martha said. There were tears in her eyes. She wiped them with the tips of her fingers.

I looked at Aunt Ivy in confusion at the strange words.

"It means she was born with an angry fighting spirit inside her," Aunt Ivy said. She sounded as if she was angry too.

"She has been gone so many years," Grandma Martha said. "But sometimes I still imagine I see her out of the corner of my eye. Now with you here, it is as if she has come back."

I looked around almost expecting the shadowy image of my mother to step out from a dark corner. Aunt Ivy just frowned at me.

Later Aunt Ivy opened the door to my little room. "You must wear something warm to bed," she said. "The heat doesn't reach much beyond the stove."

"I'll fill a hot-water bottle for you to sleep with," Grandma Martha said. I felt embarrassed over all the fuss Grandma Martha and Aunt Ivy made. No one had ever fussed over me before, and I wished they would just leave me alone.

I put on long underwear beneath my nightgown. From the small bed, I could look out the window without sitting up straight. The rain stopped. The clouds blew apart, and the sky to the east glowed.

Standing outside the door to my room, I heard Grandma Martha say to Aunt Ivy, "Go and say good night to her. Try to make her feel she is welcomed."

Aunt Ivy came and sat beside me. "Clearice, I'm sorry about your mother. She is my sister, but I never understood her unhappiness. But it seemed to spread from her to everyone around her. I thought when she met your father, and he took her to new places, she would be satisfied."

"My father calls me Clearie." I didn't tell her I could remember my mother using my full name.

"We will call you Clearie, if you want," she said.

"It's what I'm used to."

Out the window the light seemed to grow. The moon began to rise above the bay. The light made a path across the water leading to my window. "The moon," I said. "It looks like it's coming straight into this room."

"This is, October, *Dis atl-an,* month of the big moon," Aunt Ivy said.

Then I heard Grandma Martha say in a hushed voice, "Samuel, it's the devil's night. You must lock the door."

Devils? I wondered, but in my exhaustion, the even

sound of waves lulled away any fears that tried to take shape.

The bolt sliding across metal and wood was the last thing I heard. Light from the moon flooded my new room, and only my nose was still cold as I fell asleep.

2

CLOUDY SKY

Goos'

Over the next couple of days I spent much of my time in the little alcove room staring out the window. I watched how the bay constantly changed with the tides and wind. Often there were eagles sliding on the air currents and occasionally grabbing a fish from between the waves. It seemed that whenever I came out, Grandma Martha, Aunt Ivy, and even Uncle Samuel looked at me as if they were waiting for me to tell them something. But I didn't know what. It made me feel strange. My father never expected me to talk to him. He told me what to do, and that was the end of it.

Early Sunday morning Grandma Martha woke me saying, "It is time to get ready for church."

"I'm too tired to go," I said. I didn't even want to talk to her, let alone everyone else in the whole village.

When Grandma Martha told Aunt Ivy I was staying home, she said loud enough that I was sure to hear, "It is all right, I suppose, for today, but we attend church every Sunday. And tomorrow she begins school, tired or not."

On Monday morning when Aunt Ivy called me, I smelled cornmeal and coffee cooking on the woodstove the same as every other day. But that day I had to leave my room to go to school.

Uncle Samuel was already gone. From my window, I had watched him paddling his canoe from the beach next to the house out to where his fishing boat circled its anchor line in the bay. Several other village fishermen also traced paths in their canoes through the water like spiders casting out lines of web.

At first light, the water lay unmoving. Only the rain droplets plunked the surface, each making a growing ring in the water like a flower blossoming. The high tide brought the sea up under the house, and when I leaned out the window I could see a waving reflection of myself in the water below.

At breakfast Grandma Martha shook her head, "Samuel is too old to fish the sea. But he has no sons or nephews to pass on his boat to."

"He has a niece," I said. "Can't Aunt Ivy fish?"

"Yes," Aunt Ivy said. "Then Uncle Samuel could spend all his time carving out at his workshop." Abruptly changing the subject, she looked straight at me, "Are you ready for school?"

I thought about the other schools I had attended. With my father being in the army, we moved every couple years. I remembered swimming through seas of strange faces until I could find a quiet seat where I would be out of the way. But on army bases people were always coming and going, so no one took much notice of one new student. I realized in Tahkeen it would be different. I was frightened. My stomach hurt, and I felt sweaty and cold at the same time.

"Reverend and Mrs. Foster are looking forward to having you in class," Grandma Martha said.

When it was time to go, I didn't need instructions to find the right building. I could see it from Grandma Martha's door. So I simply walked the length of the street running down the center of the village until I came to the church — which was also the school. Reverend Foster was the preacher on Sundays and the teacher during the week.

"We always call it the church," Grandma Martha had said. "Because that's what it was first."

In spite of the cold rain, a handful of children played in the cleared area behind the church. The playground was surrounded by alder brush that separated it from the forest. An older boy dribbled a basketball, and under the porch roof two girls about my age stood talking.

As I came closer, my feet grew heavier. Everyone saw me walking toward them and stopped what they were doing to look. I stood frozen with all those eyes staring.

More than anything I wanted to run away. Even going back to Grandma Martha's would be better than these strange kids watching me.

Before I could make my legs move, one of the smaller boys ran over.

"You're Clearice. We've waited for you," he said.

Now I couldn't turn back. Slowly I followed him to the steps and looked at the older girls. Immediately, one lowered her eyes. The other stared me up and down.

"I'm Martha's granddaughter," I said. My voice sounded weak as if I was speaking through a long tunnel. "My name is Clearice, but please, call me Clearie."

For a minute no one said anything, and I felt my cheeks grow hot with embarrassment. They're not even going to talk to me, I thought.

Finally, the bold girl smiled. "We know who you are."

For another long moment I thought they would never tell me who they were. At last the same girl said, "I'm Mary Ruth. This is Violet."

Violet smiled shyly, but then quickly looked down at her feet without saying anything.

Mary Ruth was strong-looking, but short. I thought she was built like Grandma Martha. Her hair was in two braids that hung on either side of her round face. She was wearing a large sweater, knitted in shades of brown and cream. I noticed a lot of the kids had similar sweaters.

Quickly counting the other children, I realized I would be only the fourteenth student in the school.

Mary Ruth seemed to know what I was thinking. She said with a wave, "Soon you'll know them all too well."

Then a gray-haired man opened the door and said to us, "Come, it's time to begin."

There was just one large room inside with a barrel stove in the center. In front of the room, four rows of desks faced the blackboard. Behind the stove, smaller desks formed a circle. Against one wall, long wooden benches were stacked on top of one another. "Are those for church days?" I asked as we entered.

"Yes," Mary Ruth said. "Mrs. Foster teaches the little ones in the back. Here, sit by me."

I nodded. There was nowhere else to sit anyway. Violet followed us and sat on the other side of Mary Ruth.

"Welcome, Clearice," Reverend Foster said. "Your grandmother told me you'd be coming. Sit down. We'll get you started."

Mrs. Foster greeted me quickly as she tried to herd the seven younger children to their seats. Mrs. Foster looked nice in her cotton dress and with her hair pulled back into a hair net. Reverend Foster was more serious, and I could tell by the way everyone started in working that he was a strict teacher.

"Tell us how old you are," Reverend Foster said.

"I turned twelve in September," I said.

"So you and Mary Ruth will be doing the same grade," Reverend Foster said. "We only go through the eighth grade here. After that you must go to the Native high school in Sitka. Here's a math book. Let's see where you should begin."

Mary Ruth whispered to me, "I'm doing the seventh grade. Violet's only eleven." I didn't say anything.

At morning break, I asked Mary Ruth what the Native high school was.

"It's a boarding school with grades nine through twelve," she said. "You live there while you go to school."

"My brother Mark goes there." It was the first time I heard Violet speak. "We are so close to Sitka that he comes home some weekends."

"Why is it called the Native school?"

"Because it's a school only for Indians, run by the Presbyterian church. There's a different school for white kids."

"What about the school here? Is it only for Indians?" I asked.

"Indians are the only people who live here," Mary Ruth said.

She suddenly looked at me closely. My hair and eyes were a little lighter than hers, and I felt as if she was thinking maybe I didn't really belong. I was only half Indian. My father was Irish.

Aunt Ivy had said, "That's where she gets the wave in her hair and those eyes." She made it sound as if she didn't like the way I looked.

But Grandma Martha had answered, "She looks Indian enough for me."

"The Fosters' sons went to school here when they were growing up. They're not Indians," Violet said.

I felt better. Reverend Foster would have said something to Grandma Martha if there were rules against people with mixed blood like me.

"What was your old school like?" Violet asked.

The question surprised me. Did Violet really want to hear what I had to say? No one had before.

Violet was very different from Mary Ruth. She reminded me of a little bird. Her fingers were so bony, almost like tiny talons, and her thin hair straggled at her jaw as if it couldn't grow any longer. But her brown-black eyes were intense. Standing next to her I felt oversized, like a brick next to a pebble.

While I considered her question I remembered plainly the rows and rows of children I could never get up the nerve to speak to, and the halls where I could walk, touching other shoulders, but still not be seen. It was as if I was invisible. But now these two girls were waiting for my answer. "Bigger," was all I said.

I found that even though Mary Ruth was quick and good at her lessons, I could keep up with her. At lunchtime everyone went home to eat. I walked home alone but noticed Mary Ruth walking the same direction a little ahead of me. She and her brother Douglas went into a house a few doors before Grandma Martha's and on the forest side of the street.

Near the end of the day, Reverend Foster told us to study quietly so the little children could write spelling words on the blackboard. Just as they began, we heard heavy footsteps on the classroom stairs and a thud against the door. No knock. Everyone waited. Reverend Foster opened it and a man stumbled in, knocking Reverend Foster back. Mrs. Foster gasped and put her arms out as if to hold the children.

"Who's that?" I whispered to Mary Ruth. The man was trying to get to his feet, holding on to the door handle and pulling himself up unsteadily. He was short like Uncle Samuel, but stocky with a square head and squinty eyes.

"Henry Jonee," Reverend Foster said quietly. "You don't belong here. Get out now."

The serious tone in his voice frightened me.

"I came to visit the old place," Henry Jonee said. I heard an anger that made his words sound like threats. His voice was slurred.

"You're drunk," Reverend Foster said.

"Am I?" Henry Jonee said. He took a step toward Reverend Foster.

"Leave," Reverend Foster said.

"You always tried to tell me what to do. Well, not anymore." He reached out to shove Reverend Foster.

When Reverend Foster saw Henry Jonee coming at him, he grabbed Henry by his thick wool shirt and pinned him against the wall. Reverend Foster was not tall, but he was large-boned and heavy. He almost lifted Henry Jonee's feet off the floor, shoving him out the door. "I will see you when you're sober," Reverend Foster said. Henry Jonee caught himself on the stair railing; his feet crumpled under him.

We heard Henry Jonee swear back at the school as Reverend Foster bolted the door. When he was gone, I realized I was gripping the desk with both hands and my knuckles were white.

Reverend Foster took deep breaths but didn't say anything. He kept the school ten minutes late as he watched out the window until Henry Jonee wandered out of sight. With a shaky voice, Mrs. Foster read a story aloud from one of the primary readers.

Finally, Reverend Foster said we could go. This time Mary Ruth walked with me and told me about Henry Jonee.

"Tom Jonee, who has the store, is his father," she said. "Henry Jonee always made trouble. Reverend Foster kicked him out of school when he burned down the church storage shed. After that, he left the village for a long time, but then he came back. Now, he makes runs in his father's boat."

"Makes runs?" I asked.

"He buys whiskey in Sitka and brings it back to sell in the village," Mary Ruth said. "He usually brings it in on

Friday. Many people drink much then. It's the devil's night."

So that was the devil's night that worried Grandma Martha when she told Uncle Samuel to lock the door. The fear I felt when Henry Jonee stormed into the schoolroom still made my legs weak. "Why doesn't anyone stop him?" I asked.

"Some are trying to make Tahkeen a dry village where liquor is not allowed," Mary Ruth said. "Violet and Mark's father, Charlie, and Reverend Foster are trying to get everyone to agree. But many people have been drinking for so long now they will not stop."

We reached Mary Ruth's house and she said good-bye. I crossed the street toward Grandma Martha's. When I came into the house, I didn't see anyone at first. Then I noticed Aunt Ivy sitting on the floor in front of a wooden frame. Pinned on the wall, near her, was a large pattern of brown paper. There was a design drawn on it.

"Shh," she said. "Your grandmother naps."

"What are you doing?" I came up beside her.

"I am weaving a *naaxein.* It is a traditional blanket used in ceremonies."

"*Naaxein* means blanket?" I asked.

"No, just this blanket. A regular blanket is" — Aunt Ivy paused — "*l'ee.* I can't speak the old language very well."

"Will your blanket look like that?" I asked and

pointed to the finished triangular one that hung on the wall.

"Yes," she said. "But this will have a center design of the frog. That one is an eagle."

I felt the thick yarn between my fingers. It was rough and soft at the same time. Most of the wool was a creamy off-white color, but different parts of the pattern that made the eagle were colored black, blue, and yellow. It was one of the most beautiful things I had ever seen.

"Where do you get the wool?" I didn't remember seeing any sheep.

"It is the hair of the mountain goat," Aunt Ivy said. "Three white goat pelts will make a blanket. Then I use the plants of the woods to color it."

"How long have you been weaving?" I asked.

"All my life," she said.

In my imagination I saw my mother working here, beside Aunt Ivy. I would have liked to do something she had done.

With the words catching in my mouth, I quietly asked, "Did my mother weave?"

Aunt Ivy looked at me closely. "No," she said. "Dora could do nothing but complain."

I was crushed. Aunt Ivy made it clear she didn't like my mother. But I couldn't stop myself from wondering what Aunt Ivy and my mother were like when they lived here together.

Almost as if by itself, my hand reached out to feel the weaving Aunt Ivy was working on.

"What did she do?" I asked.

"Dora was always lazy and refused to try anything," Aunt Ivy said bitterly. "Besides, her thick hands were clumsy."

With those words I pulled my hand back, trying to hide its thickness. They are like my mother's, I thought. Aunt Ivy's fingers reminded me of willow twigs, long and supple.

Aunt Ivy saw me but turned again to her work. She said, sighing but without looking at me, "You see, even after so many years your mother still has the power to make me angry."

Aunt Ivy's weaving frame resembled the top half of a window without any glass in it. Fine strips of tree bark made the vertical threads. Aunt Ivy wove the yarn horizontally in and out of the bark strips.

Several piles of fine loose goat hair sat beside her. Aunt Ivy took some of the hair and began rolling it over and over on her thigh with her right hand. With the left hand she pulled an ever-growing length of fibers twisted together.

"This is how you spin the yarn," she said. "Here, you try it."

"No, I couldn't." I said. It looked hard, and I never could do anything with my hands. Now I knew it was because I was clumsy like my mother. Aunt Ivy already didn't like it that I looked like the sister she couldn't stand. I didn't want her to see I was just like her. "I have homework." And I quickly went into my room.

Later, when I came out, Aunt Ivy had two piles of brushed hair on the table. She said, "We will spin yarn tonight."

I saw Grandma Martha glance over to me from the stove. She nodded and smiled.

I understood the decision was made for me; I was to learn spinning and weaving. "I can't. I've never done anything like that."

"It is the Tlingit way," Aunt Ivy said. "Our women have always been weavers."

"My mother didn't."

"Your mother did nothing but beat us with her hate," Aunt Ivy said loudly.

"Ivy!" Grandma Martha said. She saw my tears and started toward me, but before she could get near I ran to my room and shut the door. I sat on the bed. As the tears began I put the pillow over my ears. I didn't want to know what they were saying in the other room.

3
ICEBERG

XAATL

My room felt like a raft, separate from the house and floating in a cold darkness. I thought, any minute I could be thrown off by a wave and fall into nothingness. I always knew my father hated my mother after she left. Now I learned even her own family didn't like her. And they didn't like me because I reminded them of her. I was afraid there was nothing I could do to change if I was like her.

I heard Aunt Ivy say, "Difficult." I knew that she meant me.

The rain came hard and the wind blew it against the window. The sound drowned out whatever else Aunt Ivy and Grandma Martha said in the other room. I was glad I couldn't hear. I was sure they were talking about me the same way they spoke about my mother. The way my father spoke about her.

"You just stay quiet," he had told me. "After living with that mother of yours, I don't want any more ugly-tongued females around."

After not thinking about them much, my father's angry words came back to me like the returning tide. I cried into sleep.

When I woke up everything was quiet: no rain, no wind. The house was dark. Someone had opened my bedroom door and spread a quilt over me. I sat up. The night on the bay seemed lighter, but I couldn't see the moon.

I slipped from bed and went to the front window that looked out to the village street. Everything appeared as if it was painted in light. It was snow. A thin cover of white over everything whispered "hush" to me.

I tiptoed back and pulled on my boots and coat very quietly, so as not to wake Uncle Samuel, who slept on a cot in back of the kitchen. Silently, I turned the door handle and squeezed out into the huge quiet.

The frigid cold surrounded me, and my nose burned when I took a breath. The peacefulness of the empty space felt wonderful. I walked to the beach. From across the street, a barking dog made the only noise.

At the edge of the water, the tiny waves licked at the gravel shore in a slow, even rhythm. It was as if they were calmed by a lullaby of snow. I swayed with the movement of water, imagining myself alone in the world. No one to tell me who I was.

I remembered how after my mother left, my father would often yell at me. I would stay as still and quiet as ice until he finished. Then I would go and hide from him in my closet. There it was dark. I kept one of my baby blankets to curl up on. The whole time I used to imagine I was a stowaway on an old sailing ship far out at sea, and it wasn't until the crew went to sleep that I could sneak out for food and water.

My father never looked for me.

Standing on the beach, I lifted my face and felt each snowflake that fell out of the darkness like a frozen tear. I decided that while in Tahkeen, I would turn my tears to ice and freeze my sadness inside where no one could thaw it, like the frozen statue I was with my father. Then they wouldn't be able to see how much I was like my mother.

In the morning when I heard Grandma Martha start the fire in the cookstove, I got up and put on my blue jumper and warm stockings.

When I came out of my room Grandma Martha and Uncle Samuel both looked at me with concern in their eyes.

Aunt Ivy said briskly, "Niece, you are to set the table."

I did my chore without saying a word. I just kept telling myself, "I am frozen, I am frozen."

During the week we fell into a pattern. I tried to find things to do that kept me out of Aunt Ivy and Grandma Martha's way. Most of the time I studied or read books borrowed from Mrs. Foster. The silence between us was a quiet sea and I floated in it like an iceberg, only occasionally bumping briefly into someone else.

Every night Aunt Ivy sat and slowly wove yarn into her frame. Uncle Samuel carved, showering the floor with small slivers. Grandma Martha rocked and knitted. This was my signal to open a book and read to myself at the table. Sometimes I would hear Uncle Samuel telling the old stories of the Tlingit clans in a singsong voice, stories about Raven and Killer Whale. I tried not to listen, but his words entered my brain no matter how hard I worked to keep them out.

One evening, just after Uncle Samuel had finished a story, Aunt Ivy said to me, "You must write to your father. He will want to know how you get on."

I had written him a very short note when I arrived. But now I sat for a long time with the empty paper in front of me. "I don't know what to say," I told Aunt Ivy.

"Tell him what you see and hear," Grandma Martha said.

Before I knew what was happening I wrote every word of the story Uncle Samuel had just finished.

Dear Father,

It does rain a lot in Tahkeen. And the fog comes in almost every night. It covers the water like a blanket. Uncle Samuel says it is the Fog Woman. He says she was the wife of Raven and she made salmon in a magic basket, which fed the people. But one day Raven forgot how much his beautiful wife did for him. He argued with her and hit her with a piece of dried salmon. She ran away, taking all the fish with her. When Raven chased her and tried to grab her, his hand went right through her body like mist. She ran into the water with all the salmon, and we see her today as fog. Even though Fog Woman took all the fish with her into the sea, we still eat it every night.

Your daughter,
Clearie

Two weeks later, after class on Friday, Violet's brother Mark was home from high school in Sitka. He waited on the steps to walk with her. Violet quietly introduced us, though I knew who Mark was because Violet talked about him all the time.

"Violet told me you came," he said. "How are you liking life in Tahkeen?" Mark's dark hair was parted on the side. It was longer than I was used to seeing. One piece fell down over the center of his forehead when he talked. I couldn't help looking at his brown eyes, crinkling a little at the corners when he smiled.

I thought about keeping myself frozen from Grandma Martha, Uncle Samuel, and Aunt Ivy, and it was suddenly difficult to make my mouth move. "It's different," I said.

"Have you looked around at all since you've been here?" He asked. "Gone upriver, to Seigan Island?"

Although my head was full of words wanting to come out, I could only shake my head no.

"We'll have to take her, Violet," he said. "And Mary Ruth, you should come along."

When Mark said he wanted to take me some place I was so surprised I couldn't think. Then, I thought, I can't go with him. I wouldn't know what to say or do.

Reverend Foster put his head out the door and greeted Mark. "I hope you're sticking to your schoolwork over there in the big city."

"Yes, sir," Mark said. "As always."

"Your sister is going to fly right by you, if you aren't careful. She's one of the brightest students I've ever had."

Violet blushed and looked at her feet at hearing Reverend Foster's praise. But Mark smiled with pride.

Mrs. Foster joined us, saying, "Mark, it's nice to see you back."

On the way home Mary Ruth chatted on and on, but I couldn't listen. My mind was on Mark.

As we passed the dock where I first landed in Tahkeen, I noticed that Mary Ruth had stopped. She stood staring at a small group of people standing out at the edge. They all looked down the bay with their backs to Mary Ruth and me.

"They wait for Henry Jonee," Mary Ruth said. There were four or five men and two women. I didn't recognize anyone in the group and started to go.

"Are you coming?" I asked.

Mary Ruth didn't answer but walked up to the crowd and pulled on the sleeve of a large man.

"Don't stay here. Come home," she said to him. The man looked down at Mary Ruth, but he didn't seem to hear her words.

Watching them I had a sudden memory of my mother. It must have been just before she left, when I was five years old. I saw her sitting at the table in our apartment. I was holding on to her sleeve and crying, "Please, Mama, please." Even though her face turned toward me, it was as if I wasn't there.

The memory ended when I saw the other people on the dock laugh. The man Mary Ruth clung to pushed her away and said, "Get!" As she stepped back, the heel of Mary Ruth's shoe caught in the uneven boards of the dock and she fell. When she landed her dress pushed up around her waist, showing her long winter woolens. The group laughed harder. I rushed over to help her. She was crying and her face was very red.

"Come to my house," I said.

Mary Ruth let me lead her into the house. When Aunt Ivy and Grandma Martha saw Mary Ruth's tears, Grandma Martha said, "I'll boil tea." Aunt Ivy brought out a plate of cookies bought from the store as a special treat. We sat across from Mary Ruth.

"James again?" Aunt Ivy asked.

Mary Ruth nodded. "Please don't tell my mother."

"Irtha will know soon, if she doesn't already," Aunt Ivy said.

"He promised her he would not go tonight. There is still time for him to change his mind before Henry Jonee comes," she said.

"Who was he?" I asked.

"My father," Mary Ruth said.

Later, when I was getting ready for bed, I heard the noise of people somewhere outside. I thought of Mary Ruth waiting for her father to return from the devil's night. As I climbed into bed and pulled the blankets around me, I again saw myself crying and pleading with my mother.

4 Devil's Club

S'axt

Sometime later a splintering noise woke me. In sleep it sounded far off. Through the noise I dreamed I was back in our apartment. The outline of my mother was visible in the next room as if I were looking through a transparent wall. My vision was of her twirling in the middle of our living room like a cyclone. The wind she stirred sent lamps, furniture, and pictures flying around and around until they shattered against the walls.

I sat up and heard the noise again. Awake, I knew I was in the alcove room suspended above the bay at Tahkeen. The crashing was breaking glass. Without sleep to filter the noise it sounded much closer. From somewhere down the beach I heard angry voices.

At that same moment Grandma Martha came down

the stairway. Aunt Ivy's quicker steps followed. Grandma said, "Samuel, wake up. There is something going on in the village."

I pulled on socks and a sweater. Aunt Ivy went outside, trying to look down the beach. "I can't see anything."

Uncle Samuel put on wool trousers and a shirt over his long underwear. He stepped into his boots without tying them. "Stay here. I will go."

Grandma Martha and I joined Aunt Ivy outside the door. We watched Uncle Samuel's small silhouette, black against light, walk away.

From behind, three men pushed past us, heading toward the noise. They smelled like liquor. "Hooch," Grandma Martha said, fanning her hand in front of her nose.

When the men were gone, Aunt Ivy said, "I'm sure Henry Jonee sells his whiskey at the beach tonight. They will quiet down soon. Let's wait inside for Uncle Samuel."

As we turned to go back in I saw someone across the road moving around one of the old deserted houses. He had a large can or jug in his hand. It looked as if he was dumping out whatever was in it onto the ground. Suddenly he stood up and his face was in the dim light. He looked over toward where I stood a little in front of Aunt Ivy. I couldn't tell if he could see me or not.

That looks like Henry Jonee, I thought, the man who had burst into the school drunk! Just as quickly he leaned down again.

Before I could give it much thought, Grandma Martha was shooing me in through the door. Back inside, Aunt Ivy opened the barrel stove and stirred the coals, then placed several pieces of wood on the tiny flames.

"I'll boil tea," Grandma Martha said.

The tea water wasn't even hot when Uncle Samuel burst through the door, "The old house across the street is burning! Hurry, we must leave."

"Leave?" Grandma Martha asked.

"I'll take you to the Fosters," Uncle Samuel said. "Quickly! The fire could spread."

I thought to myself, Why do we have to go? Won't the fire department put it out? But before I could ask, there was a rapid knock.

"It's Irtha. Let us in," Mary Ruth's mother said through the door. Aunt Ivy opened it a small way into the darkness. Mary Ruth, her mother, and brother slid inside, wearing rubber boots and nightclothes, watching behind them as if being chased.

"The whole village will burn," Irtha said.

"Come, we will go down to the church together," Aunt Ivy said as she gathered coats and blankets in her arms.

"When the fire started I was dreaming that James came home and his body was in flames," Irtha said. "His arms and legs blazed. His head burned like a candlewick. I could just see the outline of his head within the orange glow like a shadow. I woke up to this fire outside."

Grandma Martha took a blanket from my bed and placed it around Irtha's shoulders. She kept her hands on the woman as if to push the fear down. Irtha cried, "I am afraid James will die."

"We must go!" Aunt Ivy said.

Holding as much as we could carry we rushed down toward the church. Other people were leaving their homes or watching the fire from their doorways. The church bell rang a warning.

In the street we met Reverend Foster, Mark, and his father, Charlie, heading toward us. They were pulling a cart with hoses and a machine in it. "We have the fire pump," Reverend Foster said to Uncle Samuel. "We must find everyone who can help. Maybe even people from down at the beach, if they're not too drunk."

"It will sober them up quickly," Charlie Hosket said. "There is no use trying to save the empty house that burns. We must protect everything else."

"Go ahead, Martha," Reverend Foster said. "Mrs. Foster will help you get comfortable in the church."

Aunt Ivy handed over the bundle she carried to Grandma Martha. "I'm going to help with the fire."

"No," Uncle Samuel said. "The women must be safe at the church."

"We'll need everyone who is able," Reverend Foster said.

"I am able," Aunt Ivy said, glaring at Uncle Samuel.

He didn't say anything more.

I started to follow Grandma Martha to the church but Aunt Ivy caught my sleeve. "You come with us."

"She's only a child," Grandma Martha said.

"She's big enough to start being useful," Aunt Ivy said.

I couldn't imagine how I could help. I'd never done anything like fight fires. "I don't know what to do," I said. "Why can't the fire department put it out?"

Aunt Ivy gave me an angry look. "*We* are the fire department."

I followed, while the others maneuvered the cart down to the beach below our house. Mark and his father attached the hoses to the machine. One hose ran into the sea. The other was dragged up the bank toward the fire.

"Get over there," Aunt Ivy told me. "We pump." She pointed to one end of the cart while she climbed into the other. On top of the pump was a seesaw with two handles. Aunt Ivy grabbed one so I took the other. The first few pumps were easy, but when water from the bay entered the hoses the work became hard. Within a minute my arms ached and I felt as if I couldn't breathe.

"I can't do this," I said. "It's too hard."

"Don't stop," Aunt Ivy commanded. "Our homes could burn."

But my mind screamed, I can't — I can't do anything! The air became smoky as the fire grew, glowing around the dark shape of the other buildings. Strange arms of flame, orange, yellow and blue, slashed out into the air.

"Keep pumping, keep pumping," Aunt Ivy said as she worked. I tried to focus on what she was saying, but my mind was louder.

Then ashes, some still glowing alive and red, began raining down on us from the thick sky. They fell on our hands and clothes and in our hair.

I stopped pumping and madly tried to brush the cinders out of my hair. "They're burning me," I screamed jumping down from the cart and frantically swatting at my head.

Aunt Ivy came over to me. "Stop it," she cried, grabbing me by the shoulders. "Keep pumping."

"I can't do it!" I said, crying. "It's too hard." The air was so smoky my eyes burned. I wanted to lie down on the rocks and cover my face. "I'm not strong enough."

"You must be," she said.

"I don't know how," I sobbed.

"Here," Aunt Ivy said, and pointed to my head. "Your strength comes from here. In your mind. If you think strong, you can do anything." She dragged me back to the cart.

"Leave me alone. You hate me just like you hated my mother!" I cried. While inside my head I kept hearing, Stay frozen, don't let her see I'm like my mother, weak and worthless.

"I don't hate you," Aunt Ivy said more softly. "I need you to help me, please. Pumping, pumping, pumping. Say it out loud, Clearie."

I tried, but my arms hurt and the smoke made my lungs burn, "Pumping," I said quietly.

"Be strong," Aunt Ivy said. "I know it's in you."

"Pumping, pumping, pumping," I said. Then I heard it in my brain, pumping, growing from a whisper. As the sound in my head became louder, my arms felt stronger. A smoother rhythm moved within me and my chest loosened so I could breathe.

Each stroke became easier. I watched Aunt Ivy to match her motions and speed.

I don't know how long we worked, moving water through the hose, but suddenly it began to rain. Almost instantly the heavy drops cleared the air. I took deep whiffs to suck the cold freshness as far into my lungs as I could.

"The rain will help," Aunt Ivy said. "It won't be much longer now."

She was right. A few minutes later the glow of the fire shrank almost out of sight behind our house. Mark came down the beach. "You can stop. It won't spread now."

Aunt Ivy and I let our legs collapse. We sat on the edge of the cart. My arms felt as if they were rubber and my muscles quivered. Aunt Ivy leaned over her knees and whispered, "It's over. You did well, niece."

The words were said so quietly but I tried to hold them like a deep breath. I didn't answer her. Instead I looked down at my hands. The skin was rubbed off, forming hot blisters on each palm. From the rocks I scooped up a handful of slushy snow. The warmth of my hands melted it.

"Let's go home," Aunt Ivy said.

Now that the fire was going out, I was ashamed of how I had screamed and cried. Why couldn't I have acted more like Aunt Ivy? She was so strong and in control the whole time. I didn't deserve her praise.

We hauled our exhausted, wet bodies up the bank to the house. Grandma Martha came back from the Fosters. She helped Aunt Ivy and me take off our wet things and wrapped us in blankets. "I'll boil tea," she said. Nothing ever tasted so good as that hot, sweet liquid.

Finally, Uncle Samuel stumbled through the door. "It is almost out. Just smoke left," he said. Grandma Martha rushed to make him comfortable.

"What happened to the people we heard on the beach?" I asked.

Aunt Ivy shrugged her shoulders. "I suppose they finally went home."

"Irtha left Fosters as soon as the rain started, to be home when James came back," Grandma Martha said.

"It would be better if she stayed away, with James feeling the hooch," Aunt Ivy said.

"There were some very drunk people before the fire began," Uncle Samuel said. "And some were fighting. I saw them throw bottles and stones."

"How do you think the fire started?" Grandma Martha asked.

"I don't know," Uncle Samuel said.

The picture of Henry Jonee came rushing back to me. He could have started the fire. I saw him there just moments before. But I wasn't sure and was afraid to say anything.

"For those fighting, there will be many achy heads and bruises tomorrow," Aunt Ivy said. She looked out the window toward where the fire had been. "We should try to sleep."

"What time is it?" I asked.

Grandma Martha held the small windup clock near the lamp. "It is almost three o'clock." There were not many hours left before dawn.

I went back to bed and sat looking out the window. The tide was still low and someone walked through the gravel on the beach below my room.

In the morning, while I lay in bed, I heard Uncle Samuel say he was going to walk down to where the fire had been.

"I may find some wood that can be salvaged," he said.

I slowly pushed myself out of bed, every part of my body groaning and stiff. I was curious to see if any of the house was still there after the fire. I leaned into the other room.

"Can I go along?" I asked.

"Get dressed," Grandma Martha said.

I walked with Uncle Samuel over to the house that had burned, near the tribal house.

The tribal house was the only structure built in the old style, when groups of several families lived together. Both the walls and roof were made of wide wood planks nailed side by side. No one lived in the house, but Uncle Samuel said it was used for ceremonies and some meetings. Across the outside, painted Tlingit designs flew and floated on the walls. In front was a carved pole, twice as tall as the building, with a beaver sitting on the top.

"When I was a young man, I helped to carve that pole," Uncle Samuel said. "Many men worked together to build this house of our people."

I looked up at the pole. The fire had come within fifty yards of the tribal house. If the wind had been blowing or the rain had not come, it easily might have ignited the building. From there it could have spread throughout the village.

"It's lucky the night was calm," I said.

"Yes," Uncle Samuel said. "To the north, in the village of my grandmother, there was once a great fire that burned everything. When the wind blows the flames, you cannot fight against them. She told me all the people stood in the cold river and watched their homes burn." He looked at the tribal house as he spoke.

We walked around the charred remains of the burnt house. As we came around the back corner I spotted a large red can half hidden under a blackened timber. I picked it up. It said gasoline across the front. The picture was suddenly perfectly clear in my mind — Henry Jonee pouring gasoline around the base of the old house.

"I saw Henry Jonee with this in his hand last night," I said.

"That is bad," he said. "We must tell the Reverend what you saw."

Down at the beach where people had been drinking, we saw evidence of the fighting. Broken glass and long dried stalks of some kind of plant lay scattered around.

Uncle Samuel saw the plants and said, "Devil's Club."

I looked at the fine hairs that covered the dried woody plant stem. They looked soft, but when I ran my finger over the stem the tiny sharp spines stuck my skin and stung as if I had slapped a rock.

"If you hit someone with the Devil's Club it leaves many painful thorns in their skin," he said.

When we climbed up the bank again we met Reverend Foster helping someone out of the tribal house. It was Mary Ruth's father, James.

“I found him huddled in the corner. Passed out on the dirt floor,” Reverend Foster said. “He’s lucky it didn’t freeze last night. I’ll take him home.”

As they started down the street I summoned my courage and said, “Reverend Foster, I have something important to tell you.”

Tomorrow

Seigan

5

After Reverend Foster helped James into his house, I told him about glimpsing Henry Jonee with the gas can. Uncle Samuel stood beside me.

"Are you sure it was Henry?" he asked.

"Yes, I saw him!"

"And you saw him light the fire?"

"I saw him with the gas can in his hand. A few minutes later the house was burning," I said. "What else could have happened?"

"It's not the first time Henry has done something like this," Reverend Foster said.

That's right, I thought. Mary Ruth said that Henry Jonee had burned the church shed. As Uncle Samuel and I walked back to the house I felt as if I had done something important.

Later, when we were cleaning up the breakfast dishes, someone knocked. I opened the door and there stood Mark. He sat down at the table and fell into conversation with Uncle Samuel about the fire. My stomach fluttered hard, but when he ignored me it sank like a water-soaked log.

I went back to washing dishes. A few minutes later I heard Mark say to Uncle Samuel, "I thought Clearie might like to go upriver with me today. Maybe do a little fishing."

Suddenly my muscles jumped in excitement. I looked over and saw Uncle Samuel nod in his usual quiet way.

Grandma Martha said, "Dress warm."

I ran to get ready so fast that I forgot my shyness until we were alone outside.

"Where's Violet?" I asked as we walked toward the beach through wet snow mixed with mud.

"She's helping Mother sew," he said. "Violet said she would see you in church tomorrow."

We walked to the beach across from Mark's house where his canoe sat and climbed in. A cold breeze was blowing. Several holes in the clouds showed bits of blue. But as Mark paddled south around the end of the point and turned up river, a wall of gray fog met us.

Mark seemed at ease while I sat tense in my seat, trying to think of anything to say. He moved the boat so gracefully. Watching each deep stroke of the paddle reminded me of how the eagles I saw from my window used their wings as they swooped and glided over the bay.

Mark pulled on a rope that raised a tattered cotton sail up a small mast. Then he repeated the process on another sail right next to the first. He loosened the ropes so the sails spread out over the edge on either side of the boat like sheets on a clothes line.

"Today, we ride in the wind," he said.

Everything was still for a few moments. Then we came into the breeze. The sails flapped and filled. The houses slipped away behind the hill that formed the mouth of the river.

As we went Mark talked about some of the many times he had made this same trip. Thirty minutes later, the fog thinned and I could see steep hillsides climbing away from a widening river valley. The trees lining the banks were cottonwood, now bare with the coming of winter. A litter of gold-brown leaves lay at the base of each trunk.

The most amazing thing was that on every branch of every cottonwood sat a bald eagle. Not two or three, as I had seen from my window in the village, but hundreds all together.

"This is where the eagles meet for their big potlatch every fall," Mark said.

"What's a potlatch?" I asked, glad to have Mark lead the conversation.

"Big party," he said. "The birds come to feed on the late salmon run. I'll show you."

He pulled the sails down and paddled the boat to a place on the shore where a finger of water dug into the river bank. When we entered a dozen eagles flapped into the air, reluctantly leaving the dead fish they were eating. As the river became shallow, water became fish. So many fish squirmed and struggled beneath us that the boat skimmed across the tops of their reddish skin; fish to fish to fish like a cobblestone road. Mark put his hand into the scaly stew and pulled one into the boat.

"That is the strangest fish I've ever seen," I said. "It has teeth and a beak!"

"It's a chum salmon. But it's ready to spawn — lay its eggs. The fish leave the sea and return to the river where they were born to reproduce. They change into this along the way. Then they lay their eggs and die."

"It's so ugly. Can you eat them like this?"

"You can eat them almost up to this point. But dead fish is the main dish at the eagle's potlatch. Look!" He pointed further up the river bank. A bear was also eating one of the fish. I jumped, startled. But Mark calmly said, "Eagle invites all the other animals to the feast: bear, wolf, fox, raven."

"Shouldn't we get out of here?" I gripped the sides of the boat, ready to jump if the bear came near.

"He's too far away and too happy with his dinner to

bother with us," Mark said. As I looked again the bear picked up the fish and ambled off into the trees.

After a few minutes Mark began to back the boat out of the inlet and into the main river channel. It was narrower now, and he worked hard pushing the paddle against the current. I saw a hill of brown grass in the middle of the river ahead of us.

"Seigan Island," he said.

"What does *Seigan* mean?"

"Tomorrow," Mark said. "In the old days the powerful men of the village would come here the day before an important event — a hunting trip or a battle. They believed that from the top of the hill, they could see what tomorrow would bring."

The bow of the canoe scraped bottom, and Mark waded in the ankle-deep water to pull it far enough on shore. The island was tiny, just a stony beach surrounding a pointed hill.

"I'll build a fire so we can roast a fish," he said.

My face must have clearly shown my feelings about the fish we had just seen because Mark smiled and said, "I'll catch one still fit to eat."

We gathered dry sticks and dead grass to kindle the small flame under the wood. Mark pulled his fishing pole out of the canoe and began casting the line far out into the current.

While he fished I climbed the triangular hillside to the

top. Up there the wind felt different and fresh. In the distance I could see the bay and the tangy smoke rising from chimneys in the village.

At that moment, as if the wind brought a message from somewhere, all the eagles rose in unison from the trees and began to soar in large circles around me. I felt as if I could join them. One step off the tip of dirt where I stood and I too would be in the wind. I would fly. Maybe I could even fly high enough to see my own tomorrow.

Below, I heard Mark calling. He held a large fish in his hand. I scrambled down and watched him clean the fish on a log. By the time the fish cooked it was well past lunch time and I was very hungry, so it tasted good.

"Do you like it here?" Mark asked.

We sat close to the fire, out of the wind. "It takes some getting used to," I answered. "When I lived with my father he was always busy. He's a supply officer for army commissaries. That's the store on base."

"What did you do while your father worked?" Mark asked.

Hours alone with my radio and my books filled my memory. But I told Mark, "I was busy taking care of things at home for my father. It's harder to come here and live with so many people around."

"My mom said that Martha was very glad your father was sending you to them."

"I don't think they feel that way anymore," I said, thinking of us as frozen pieces of ice.

Mark shrugged. "I believe it's a new life for them." Then he changed the subject. "It would be exciting to see different places like you have. The farthest I've ever been is to Juneau."

"My boat stopped there before coming to Tahkeen," I said.

"After I finish school I'm going to go someplace far away, like Seattle or maybe even California." I watched his eyes sparkle excitedly as he talked.

"Seattle's not so great. My father took me there once," I said, trying to sound at ease. Mark talked to me like I was someone his own age, a friend. But with every word out of my mouth I was afraid I'd make a mistake and ruin everything.

Between glances at Mark I kept an eye on the birds above us. As I watched, there were gunshots. In my line of vision one of the dark shapes began to fall. Mark and I watched the eagle plunge into the river several hundred yards out from us and disappear into the flow of water. As I saw the beautiful bird die I felt a huge sadness flow through me.

Mark stood up to watch the brown form float away downstream. He looked angry.

There were several more shots, and another bird began to fall. This time we saw the bird fall into the willow brush on the other side of the river. Mark scanned the far shore, trying to determine where the shots were coming from.

"Help me put out the fire," he said. "We've got to stop whoever's shooting."

We threw wet sand on the flames to smother them and collected our things. Once we were in the canoe, he paddled hard across to the shore.

When we landed he scrambled up the steep bank. He looked up and down the shore. I climbed up after him.

"There's a trail," Mark said. I ran close behind him, crashing through the bushes when the trail narrowed. We came into a small clearing where a fire was still burning inside a circle of rocks. There were logs placed around the fire pit to sit on. Everywhere, glass covered the ground. Whole unbroken whiskey bottles lay on top of a carpet of ground glass shreds. Other garbage and empty rifle cartridges littered the area.

"This must be where people drink," I said.

"Stupid drunkards," Mark said.

"Why would they shoot eagles?" I asked.

"They'd shoot anything when they're drunk," he said. "Just like they probably set the old house on fire. I'm surprised they don't shoot each other."

I remembered Henry Jonee by the old house. "But birds don't hurt anyone."

"Too many Tlingits have forgotten we must share our

lives with the birds, the bears, the salmon," Mark said. "Instead we think like the white man. They say the eagle steals fish that belong only to people."

"Surely not all whites believe in shooting harmless animals?" I hoped he didn't think I might, because I was part white.

He looked at me like he was thinking how to answer. "Too many. The government will pay a two-dollar bounty for every eagle shot," Mark said. "To get paid you hand over the bird's chopped-off feet."

We heard a rustle in the brush. Henry Jonee walked into view with a rifle over his shoulder. He looked at Mark and sneered, "What do you want?" He glanced my way but spoke to Mark.

"Were you shooting eagles?" Mark said.

"Maybe I need the cash," Henry said. "What of it?"

"They are part of who you are," Mark said.

Henry spit on the ground near Mark's feet.

"That's crap left over from old times, long gone." He raised his gun and shot into the air, toward the distant birds.

Mark rushed at Henry and grabbed the gun. He flung it far into the bushes.

"You'll pay for that," Henry Jonee said. He punched Mark on the cheek. Mark pushed him hard. Henry fell into the broken glass, cutting his elbow on several sharp pieces.

“Come on, let’s go,” Mark said to me. We started to walk away.

“I’ll get you for this,” Henry yelled. “And you too, girl.” I looked back at him clutching his bleeding arm. His face held more than anger; it overflowed with hate. Not only for Mark but for me as well. Then I knew for sure Henry Jonee had started the fire. And he knew I had seen him there.

6 Change to Winter

Taakw

Mark pushed the canoe into the river's current.

"Henry Jonee is a fool. He thinks his father's wealth gives him power to do whatever he wants, no matter what it does to others," Mark said.

"I saw his face, the way he looked. Why does he hate you?"

"I guess because my father, along with the Reverend, wants to put him out of business," Mark said. "My father believes it's his personal mission to keep every person in Tahkeen on the right path."

"What do you think?"

Mark shrugged. "I don't really care what the fools do to themselves, as long as they leave me alone. It's not my job to save them."

He didn't say anything else, but stared at the movement of water around him. I could feel his anger melting away as the river rocked the boat. Mark's face began to relax. A calmness set in. It was as if the water seeped into his veins, like hot sweet tea.

"Your Uncle Samuel once told me that the river was the blood of God," Mark said.

"Uncle Samuel told you that?" I asked. I could see in my mind Uncle Samuel sitting in his chair carving and telling a story. And I had tried to keep from hearing his words saying to myself, Stay frozen.

"Long ago in the myth time the river could speak and the people understood the language of the water." He spoke Uncle Samuel's words.

Then I remembered the story of fog woman that I had written about to my father. When I had asked Uncle Samuel what the story meant he had said, "Niece, you must listen deep inside you, to where the old language still lives, to know."

At the time I didn't let myself ask any more or think about what he had said. But now, hearing Mark speak about Uncle Samuel, I was sorry I hadn't paid more attention.

"All this life flowing right past our feet." Mark said. He pointed to where several eagles waded in the water, feeding on fish.

"What does that mean?" I asked.

"Samuel says the river and the sea give us food and water. But they also take care of us in ways you can't see."

"In what way?" I asked.

"They fill our spirits like air fills our lungs. That is how ideas get started," Mark said.

"Like painting pictures or like Uncle Samuel's wood carvings?"

"Sure, but even more than that," Mark said. "Isn't this a wonderful feeling right now, floating with the current? It's like the river is holding us in the palm of its great hand."

I had never heard anyone talk like that before, or look at the world around them as Mark did. Sitting in the canoe with the soft swish of water and wind sweeping past was like being gently hugged.

Low in the bottom of the boat we sat watching the movement of the water until we reached the entrance to the bay where the river stretched into the salt water.

"Do you want to paddle?" Mark asked.

"I'll try." I thought of my blisters from the fire pump and put on my gloves to cover them.

"It's a good thing to know how to do here," he said.

We carefully traded places, Mark on one side, me on the other, sliding past one another in a slow balancing act. I held the wooden paddle the way I had seen him do and quickly dipped it into the water. The stroke was too shallow and a spray of freezing drops hit me in the face. I wiped them off.

Mark laughed. “Try again.”

I took a deeper stroke and was surprised how hard I had to push to move the canoe forward. Mark made it look so easy.

“That’s right,” he said. “Watch the bow of the boat and aim it toward where you want to go. Switch your paddle to the other side if you drift. That will keep you going in the right direction.”

I paddled all the way to the beach by the Hoskets’ house. Mark jumped out and landed the boat. My arms were tight and sore when I stepped onto the beach. I rubbed them and tried to stretch the cramped muscles.

Mark smiled and said, “You’ll have to keep doing it if you want it to get easier.”

“At least I’m warm,” I said.

Unloading our things from the canoe, I realized I didn’t feel so nervous around Mark anymore. My stomach didn’t even flip-flop when he said, “It’s getting late. I’ll take you home.”

When we reached the house it was almost dark, although it was only late afternoon. I stopped at the door and said, “Thanks. I had a wonderful time.”

“Let’s do it again,” he said.

Inside, Uncle Samuel, Aunt Ivy, and Grandma Martha sat at opposite ends of the room with the lines and equipment from Uncle Samuel’s boat spread everywhere between them. They were coiling the ropes into neat piles.

Aunt Ivy was speaking with a hard voice, "What if something were to happen to you? How would we make a living? I am young still, and strong. I could learn.

"It is not right," Uncle Samuel said.

"But if I know nothing, someday we might have to leave Tahkeen and work in the fish canneries."

Their conversation stopped as they saw us. Grandma Martha said to Mark, "Stay to eat with us."

"My mother has dinner waiting for me," Mark said. "Samuel, we'll work after church tomorrow?"

Uncle Samuel nodded.

After Mark was gone, I couldn't resist asking, "What are you working on with Mark?"

"*Kooteeyaa*, carved pole. I am teaching him."

"A totem pole?"

"*Kooteeyaa*," Uncle Samuel said. I knew he wanted me to use the Tlingit name. I didn't say it. They would have thought I cared. But after listening to Mark, I secretly said it over in my head several times.

I started to go to my room. Aunt Ivy said to me, "We could use your help here." Then she and Grandma Martha looked at each other.

Grandma Martha said, "We are putting all fishing things away. It is *taakw*, the change to winter. No more fishing until spring."

"Now I will carve," said Uncle Samuel. "Ivy thinks I should carve my own *kaa daakeidi*." He translated for me, "That is a man's grave marker."

"Uncle Samuel, I do not. I want to learn to fish and run the boat as you would have a nephew do."

So that is what they were talking about when I came in. Aunt Ivy wanted to fish with Uncle Samuel. At least they weren't talking about me.

"How was your trip upriver, Granddaughter?" Grandma Martha asked. Uncle Samuel grunted, to show he knew his sister was trying to change the subject.

"We saw Henry Jonee shooting at bald eagles," I said. "Mark argued with him about it and they almost got into a fight." I didn't mention that Henry hit Mark.

"Henry Jonee is like a huge wave that rolls in and covers this village with sadness," Grandma Martha said.

"He should go away," Aunt Ivy said.

"No one drank before Henry Jonee came?"

"Oh yes, there have long been the problems of whiskey. But it was not so easy for many people to get drunk all at once, before Henry Jonee brought in hooch to sell. Now he gets rich on many families' sorrow. And we lock our doors against our neighbors."

"Like Mary Ruth's family," I said.

"Oh, I forgot," Aunt Ivy said. "There was a package for you at the store today. From your father." She handed me a small box wrapped with paper and string. Seven Japanese stamps filled a large portion of the top. I opened it quickly. Inside was a square camera.

"It's a Brownie, that's what they're called," I said, and took it out to show everyone. The camera was about the size of a half a loaf of bread. Also in the box were three rolls of film and six flashbulbs that clipped one at a time into the center of a metal, flower-shaped flash bar. It looked a lot like the cameras newspaper photographers used in the movies, only smaller.

I took out the letter that came with it and read it quickly to myself. Grandma Martha, Aunt Ivy, and Uncle Samuel waited.

"My father never says much," I said. I read the letter to them.

Clearie,
I wanted you to have some way of remembering your time in Alaska. So as an early Christmas gift I have sent you this camera. Ask your grandmother if you can send the film to Seattle or Juneau for developing. I will send more film from the PX.

Your father

"I told you he doesn't say much," I said.

"It is enough," Grandma Martha said. "He is concerned for you."

"I'll read the instructions for the Brownie and then later I can take a picture," I said. And as if I were already snapping a photo, we were all smiling.

7 Carved Figures

Kooteeyaa

The next morning in church, when Reverend Foster finished his sermon and Mrs. Foster played a final hymn on the piano, a quiet anticipation settled over us. Now the school desks were pushed back against the wall and the wooden benches were set up in rows. The room we sat in was comfortable for fourteen students and two teachers, but with more than fifty people every corner was filled.

I looked around. I didn't know many of the faces, but Grandma Martha knew them all like her own family. It was so different here than on the army base.

I remembered my father said, "We mind our business, Clearie, and let others mind theirs. We don't want them sticking their noses into our private life." There, I always felt alone even when surrounded by people.

I suddenly remembered something else from my past. Once when my father came home, he found me out on the sidewalk with some neighbor kids. It was the first time they had ever invited me to play with them. We were being cowboys and Indians. They made me the Indian.

When my father came, the cowboys were running circles around me yelling, "Dirty, stinky Injun!"

My father's face was red. "Get inside!" he said, pushing me in front of him. "You stay away from those nosy brats. They just go home telling tales about us to their parents."

For a long time after he brought me into the house, my father sat silently at the table with his head in his hands. He never mentioned the incident again.

Now Reverend Foster was saying, "We share a common concern in Tahkeen. A problem that ties us together and steals into each and every life here."

We knew he referred to Henry Jonee and the increased drinking in the village. I had seen two of the people who were now in church waiting for whiskey on the dock last Friday. I looked around to see where Mary Ruth was. She sat with her mother and little brother, Douglas. I didn't see her father. Mark sat with Violet and their parents near the door. He was holding a book open on his lap and didn't pay any attention to the discussion.

Then I noticed Henry Jonee standing half hidden by

the doorway. Reverend Foster had been staring right at him when he spoke. I tried to watch Henry's face, but his expression stayed hidden in the shadows. Suddenly his eyes turned on me, as if he had felt me looking at him. I jumped and quickly turned around.

Mrs. Foster left her place at the piano to put the teakettle on, for after the service. When I looked again toward the door, Henry Jonee was gone.

"Because this affects us all, we need to work together for a solution," the Reverend said.

No one said anything. The hush was heavy and fearful as if the ceiling pressed the air in the room down hard against us. At last Mary Ruth's mother stood. She spoke with her head bent in a voice I could barely hear.

"Friday, my husband buys drink from Henry Jonee. He comes home and lies on the floor since yesterday. I am sorry."

I thought, how could her husband's drinking be her fault? I started to squirm in my seat. They were all sorry. I saw their faces. They believed they deserved to have their lives crushed with this. Even Grandma Martha and Aunt Ivy sat looking down at the hands in their laps like they too were guilty of something unspeakable.

Finally, Mark's father spoke up loudly, "We have to do something," he said. "Tell him he can't bring liquor into the village."

"We have told him we want him to stop, but he does

not," Mr. Simons said. He lived next to the house that had burned.

"Then we must prevent him from coming. Blockade the head of the bay. Keep him from entering," Mr. Hosket said.

Reverend Foster shook his head. "Remember the problem is not Henry Jonee. It is a deeper wound that needs healing from within us. Even if Henry Jonee stopped, someone would eventually take his place. I believe we must solve the problem as a community. Decide together that we will not drink."

Many nodded their heads in agreement. The memory of my mother's empty face as I pulled on her arm and pleaded with her rushed back to me. Now I could also remember the bottle of liquor sitting on the table beside her. Why didn't I remember it before? Somewhere inside me I had always known that she drank, but after she left, it was like I purposely forgot. It filled me with sadness. I wondered if Grandma Martha and Aunt Ivy knew about my mother's drinking. I saw a woman who had been one of those waiting on the dock leave the church. Reverend Foster also watched her go. His face looked defeated. He lowered his head and we followed him into prayer.

After the service the whole congregation stayed for coffee and tea. Mark and Violet came over to where I stood.

"Clearie, I don't have much time this afternoon,"

Mark said. "My ride back to Sitka is going around three-thirty. Why don't you come out to your uncle's shed and I'll show you what we're working on?"

I felt shy talking to Mark with so many people around us. Yesterday was easier when we were alone. Still, I couldn't help but smile at his invitation.

"Do you know where the workshop is?" he asked.

"No," I answered. "I haven't been out there yet."

"At the far end of the village, behind the tribal house, is a trail. It goes through the alders just up from the beach. The workshop is a short way down the path. You can't miss it."

"I'd like to come," I said.

Violet pointed and said, "There's Mary Ruth. I'm going to talk to her."

I thought I should go with Violet, but I wanted to stay with Mark more. "Poor Mary Ruth," I said. "While we were out on the river yesterday she was home trying to take care of her father."

"It didn't surprise me when James was found sleeping it off in the tribal house, the jerk," Mark said.

"Why doesn't Henry Jonee's father stop him from selling whiskey?" I asked.

Mark looked surprised. "You don't think Henry Jonee does this by himself? It's his father who provides the boat and fuel. Tom Jonee is as much a part of the business as his son. He's probably the one who thought of the idea.

And judging from what he charges for goods at his store, his only interest is making money."

What Mark said made sense. Even I could see it was almost as if Tom and Henry Jonee were outsiders like me, even though they had always lived here. Separated by the resentment of others, they were less a part of the community than the Fosters, who were white!

"If he's cheating people and making the whole village miserable, we should stop buying things from him," I said.

"Where would people get what they need? No one wants to return to the old days when we had nothing," Mark said.

"I don't know," I said. "But if the store had no customers, it would show Tom Jonee he couldn't go against the village."

"I wouldn't mind seeing Tom Jonee and his kid get it were it hurts," Mark said. "I wish there was some way we could pull it off."

"What if everybody went together and took turns buying supplies in Sitka?" I suggested. "My dad said that military people living in foreign countries did something like that. They made lists of items that were expensive or hard to get where they were. Then they could have one person who was going on leave buy everything and bring it back."

"Maybe we could do that," Mark said.

"Lots of people have boats. You go back and forth all the time," I said.

Aunt Ivy touched my shoulder and told me it was time to go.

Mark said, "I'll tell my father about your idea. See you later?"

As I put on my coat and started for the door I saw Mark take his father aside and say, "Clearie has an interesting idea . . ."

After changing my clothes and eating lunch, I started out to find Uncle Samuel's workshop. Uncle Samuel had gone straight from church so I carried a basket of food for him that Grandma Martha packed. I slipped my camera into it.

I walked past the tribal house. In the back where scrubby alders mixed with dead grasses, a well-used trail passed under a canopy of bushes like an arch. In the passageway, made by dense brush, the light became dim. A damp smell of swampy dirt rose through the slush.

It was just a quarter mile to the workshop, but I hurried. In my rush I saw something ahead of me, beside the trail. For a second I thought it was a bear, but then I saw, almost lost in woody growth, a group of four carved figures. One was made of wood and three were carved in light-colored stone. I recognized the figure of killer whale and wolf, but I wasn't sure what the other two represented. On the base of the stone carvings there were the years 1887, 1889 and some Tlingit words. If there was ever any writing on the wooden figure it was worn away. Later I learned they were old memorial sites, placed there to honor some past chief and left for almost seventy years.

I approached them through the wet quiet. They were beautiful. The wolf figure and I stood head-to-head. I put my hands on either side of its face and felt the cold of the stone soak through my skin. I felt that if I could hold the figure long enough, it might come alive. I wanted this animal to breathe and move, even though the carving didn't look like a real wolf but had the over-sized eyes and teeth that flowed across all Tlingit designs. This was a spot suspended in nowhere. And for some reason I felt it was mine.

Suddenly, I noticed the weight of the lunch basket and realized I had been standing there for some time. I took my camera out and snapped a picture of the statues before I ran down the trail.

Around the next bend I came to Uncle Samuel's shed, perched on the bank above the bay. A wooden slide extended from the shed to the beach where large logs could be pulled up from the water.

I knocked on the door. No one answered so I cautiously looked inside. The smell of wood filled my nose as I opened the door. Mark and Uncle Samuel bent over a long log set up on several saw horses. They were examining a spot closely and intently. They didn't even hear me. Mark ran his fingers gently around a tiny carved trough in the wood and said, "Yes, I see it."

I clicked a picture of the two of them together, at work. Uncle Samuel looked up and smiled at me. I handed him the lunch basket and he said, "Good, I am very hungry." I had never seen him look so comfortable and happy. All the lines that usually rode on his face were gone, and he spoke with confidence instead of the shy muttering I was used to.

"Mark, show my great-niece what we are doing. Tell her what it means."

I noticed that the log was not the only object in the shed. Along the walls there were intricately decorated boxes of various shapes and sizes. There were wood planks with carved designs that looked like the blanket Aunt Ivy wove, only cut in half. There were smaller carved animals like those I had seen on the statues in the woods.

"Uncle Samuel made all these things?" I asked.

"Some he did. But many of these are very old. It's just a place to keep the pieces that were done by villagers. At one time almost every man in Tahkeen worked with wood. Now there are only Samuel and me."

"Tell me about this . . ." I almost said totem pole but it didn't fit. The carving was so different and special, like the wolf figure that I found in the woods. Despite all my efforts to keep myself apart and frozen from my relatives I couldn't seem to stop myself from showing Uncle Samuel I had learned a Tlingit word. So slowly I tried pronouncing the word Uncle Samuel had said. "This *kooteeyaa* you are working on."

I looked over at him to make sure he heard me use the Tlingit word. Uncle Samuel nodded his head up and down with a grin as wide as the statue's in the woods.

At that brief moment the sight of his face sprouted a warm feeling inside my chest. Mark looked at me kindly. He said, "This pole tells the history of the eagle clan. It's your family's group, their story. Your story."

8 Canoe

Yaakw

When I said good-bye to Mark that afternoon he told me he wouldn't be back until the Christmas break began in December. Then he would have three weeks of vacation. The last thing he yelled while I watched from the dock was, "Practice paddling!" That's what I decided to do, so when he returned he would be surprised at how well I could move a boat.

When I asked Uncle Samuel if I could practice with his canoe he smiled, as he did when I spoke the Tlingit word. "Our name for canoe is *yaakw*. And yes, if the bay is quiet you can go, until it is time to help with dinner."

I was pleased, even though this only gave me an hour after school.

Through the rest of November I went out in Uncle

Samuel's canoe almost every day. The first week, one loop around the line of anchored fishing boats left the muscles in my arms burning and sore. But I enjoyed every stroke, even the painful ones. I stopped to rest often, and with my camera I took pictures of the whole village from the middle of the bay. Four or five eagles were always visible in trees along the shore or flying close over the taut surface of the water. Once I found a huge brown eagle feather, floating like a miniature canoe. I leaned out carefully and scooped it out of the water and put it in my pocket.

Not everyone understood why I loved to paddle.

"I must hurry," I told Mary Ruth as we walked home after school.

"I don't see why you want to go make circles out in the bay with your uncle's canoe," she said.

I started to answer but realized I didn't know exactly why. I knew I started because I wanted to impress Mark, but now it was more than that. I looked forward to paddling all day.

"It's fun," I said.

"Why don't you see if Samuel will get a motor skiff, like Henry Jonee's, instead of doing it the old way?" Mary Ruth asked.

Mary Ruth, without knowing it, had just told me I was doing something Indian. It felt good.

"It's great when you start to get warm and the water is

moving along with you," I said. I heard the enthusiasm in my voice.

"Well, I would want to go fast with a motor," Mary Ruth said.

By the second week of practice I started to do two laps. The weather stayed overcast but quite warm, forty degrees or more. I was comfortable paddling in my warm hat and mittens. It was dark by the final stretch, and I would follow the lines of light reflected from the windows of the houses as they held themselves out to me.

One evening, I noticed that each scoop of water my paddle disturbed was full of glowing spots. I stopped, took off my mitten, and swished my hand in the cold water. Instantly, shining particles like fireflies surrounded my fingers. The canoe itself created a cloud of light that floated for a moment in the black bay. I glided as slowly as possible toward the shore, to make every minute of moving in light last.

My cheeks were red-cold when I came into the house. The air felt hot compared to outside. The smell of fried fish filled the room like fog.

"Clearie, you have come in so late tonight," Aunt Ivy said. She was already laying out plates on the table.

"We worried," Grandma Martha said.

I was out of breath from hurrying up the bank. "There was the most amazing stuff in the water," I said. "Lights in the water. What was it?"

"It's phosphorescence. Tiny plants that give off light," Aunt Ivy said. "It appears several times a year."

"It is the watery breath of the Kushtarka," Uncle Samuel said.

Aunt Ivy laughed. "There is no such thing, Uncle Samuel. You can't still believe those old superstitions?"

"Who can really know?" Uncle Samuel said.

"The Kushtarka is half man, half land otter, that people long ago believed could change forms magically," Aunt Ivy said.

"When I was a young boy my mother would say to me, 'Samuel, you must be good because the Kushtarka will rise out of the water and snatch you away. He takes naughty children to the water world to be his slaves.'"

"Yes," Grandma Martha said. "I was so scared. If I heard a fish jump, I thought, the Kushtarka is coming, the Kushtarka is coming."

"Even now, in my boat, when I see the lights in the water I think first, it is the breath of the Kushtarka as he comes from deep down," Uncle Samuel said. "I must remind myself that my niece, who has been to school, says no, that cannot be."

Aunt Ivy laughed at Uncle Samuel's teasing.

"Oh, I know you are right, Niece. I am old and I have never seen the Kushtarka. I cannot name a single person who ever became a slave to him. But myth is strong inside me and does not die easily."

When we went to church on the first Sunday of December, Reverend Foster again spoke of the drinking problem in the village. "We are grateful that in these last weeks there has been no more trouble like the night of the fire.

"I have given our problem much thought and prayer. I believe God has rewarded me with an answer," he continued. "I ask everyone in Church to sign a letter promising they will not drink. We'll put our names here under this simple prayer: God give us strength."

On the way out of church I watched everyone stopping to put their names in neat little rows under Reverend Foster's prayer. Mary Ruth's mother held her husband's arm proudly as he added his name.

After church I heard several people talking about the idea of boycotting Tom Jonee's store. Reverend Foster nodded and said, "It was Clearie's idea."

"It would be too difficult," someone said.

"Yes," Mrs. Hosket said. "What if the sea is rough and we can't get to Sitka when we need to?"

Even Aunt Ivy and Grandma Martha were talking about it on the way home. "It is a way we can show Tom Jonee and his son that we will not tolerate the trouble they cause," Aunt Ivy said.

"But it is not the food we buy that causes the problems, daughter. It is the whiskey. The problem will go away when no one drinks," Grandma Martha said.

"It doesn't matter anyway," Aunt Ivy said. "No boycott will ever take place. It is only rumors and already people argue over the idea. They would never agree to work together. We must hope Reverend Foster's plan helps people to stop their drinking."

"I don't think Mary Ruth's father can stop," I said.

They both looked at me. "Of course he will now," Grandma Martha said. "James signed the promise in church. I saw him."

"Even a million promises aren't enough to stop him," I told them.

"Why do you say this?" Aunt Ivy asked me.

I hesitated. I didn't think they knew that my mother was like James and right now could be drunk, or dead. I thought I would start crying if I said anything.

"Why do you say that about James?" Aunt Ivy asked again.

I swallowed and looked up into the breeze so that the wind would dry my eyes. "I can remember my mother drinking like he does."

I saw Grandma Martha and Aunt Ivy's faces sadden. I realized they did know about her drinking.

"I have known people to stop," Grandma Martha said finally. "Remember Elizabeth Hoostak? For years she stayed in her house unless it was to find liquor. She did not eat or bathe herself. Then God found her."

"I remember she became terribly ill from drinking

and was in the hospital for a long time before joining the church," Aunt Ivy said.

"God saved her," Grandma Martha said.

On Sundays after church now I always took Uncle Samuel's lunch to him in his workshop. Uncle Samuel worked on his carving every day. Grandma Martha worried about him. "This year he works too much. He hurries his life."

"I don't understand," I said.

"He is afraid he doesn't have much time left to carve."

"He thinks he is going to die?" I didn't know how old Uncle Samuel was. His face looked ancient, but he couldn't be that old.

"No, he knows these years of growing old will make his work more difficult for him. It's not his own death he fears, but the death of what makes us Tlingits."

Out at Uncle Samuel's workshop I entered quietly and watched him for a few minutes while he slowly scraped away the tiny layers of wood. He looked up and smiled. "Good, it is lunch."

"You've done a lot this week," I said. "You know, Grandma Martha and Aunt Ivy are worried about you."

"This is what I have to leave behind that says our family was here."

"If you want the family to continue here, why don't you teach Aunt Ivy to fish?"

"It is not good."

"Except for Mark, isn't Aunt Ivy the only other person in Tahkeen who is still doing a Tlingit art? She's afraid she'll have to leave and work in a fish cannery, if you can't support them anymore. She told Grandma Martha that the women who work at the canneries all have to live in one big room, they can't have their own house. She said there was a lot of fighting and noise."

For a moment it looked like Uncle Samuel was really thinking about what I said. But then he blurted out, "It is not right for a woman to fish out there among so many men." He started taking items from the lunch basket without looking at me, showing he was finished with the subject.

Walking back I stopped at the carved figures in the woods. I held the wolf face and looked into the stone of its blank eyes. Aunt Ivy was the only weaver left in the village. To follow Uncle Samuel there was only Mark. I said to the wolf statue, "Someday, you may be the only thing left in Tahkeen."

9 Cold North Wind

Kusa-aat' xoon

The next week on Wednesday I could not paddle on the bay after school. The wind blew hard and cold from the north. Mary Ruth and I huddled in our coats as we hurried home in the afternoon. It was too cold even for talking.

The hillsides were spotted white where snow froze into ice patches. The water in the bay was choppy and jagged. It looked like the angry mouth of some beast snapping his teeth up out of the earth at the wind above. An icy fog rose from the water that made it look even more like a monster. It reminded me of Uncle Samuel's description of the Kushtarka.

As I neared the house my legs became numb with cold. I rushed in the door and banged it closed behind me. Aunt Ivy and Grandma Martha were both sitting by the stove knitting. They looked surprised when I came in and quickly stuffed what they were working on into Grandma Martha's basket.

"Granddaughter, you are home," Grandma Martha said. "I'll boil tea for you."

I went to stand close to the barrel stove.

"Of course the weather is too stormy for you to go out in Uncle Samuel's boat today," Aunt Ivy said. She sounded as if she was explaining to herself why I would be home early.

I could only nod to her in reply. The skin around my mouth was stiff with cold.

Suddenly I understood: Christmas. They were making me a gift and I had caught them when I came home. That is what they hid away so quickly. Before today I had hardly given the holiday a thought, but earlier, during school, Mrs. Foster helped the younger children start cutting out stars and green trees to pin up in the windows. She said we would begin practicing a Christmas program to be presented on Christmas Eve.

"*Kusa-aat xoon* blows hard on us today," Grandma Martha said. She quietly covered her knitting basket and put it behind the cookstove, out of my sight.

I realized I must think of gifts to give to Grandma Martha, Aunt Ivy, and Uncle Samuel. No matter that I tried to keep them shut out, if they gave me gifts I would have to do something in return. Even in the terrible years after my mother left, when my father and I had not celebrated much at Christmas, I always gave him some small gift I made in school. In return he would take me to the PX to choose something I wanted. This year he had sent me the camera.

When I was warmer I said, "Mrs. Foster says there is a Christmas service and program on Christmas Eve. Can we go?"

"Everyone goes," Grandma Martha said. She stirred sugar into the tea and handed it to me at the stove. "In Tahkeen the service and program is our Christmas celebration. A few days before the holiday we will join together to make bags of treats for the little children to receive when Santa visits. Christmas Eve we have church, and everyone brings food to share."

"Do you put up a Christmas tree?" I asked.

"Only in the church," Aunt Ivy said. "Here, Christmas is for children and for worship."

"We don't give gifts to the adults," Grandma Martha said.

The next day, I asked Violet and Mary Ruth about what gifts they gave their families for Christmas.

Mary Ruth said, "When fishing is good everyone gets store-bought presents from Sitka. But most years we make Christmas out of whatever we have."

"Tom Jonee is the only one with money to buy what

he likes," Violet said. "This year I am knitting socks." From her book bag she pulled out a wad of brown yarn suspended from three small wooden knitting needles.

"How do you do that?" I asked.

"It's simple. You knit around and around the triangle that the three needles make, starting from the top of the sock and ending at the toe. Only the heel is a bit tricky."

"What are you going to do, Mary Ruth?" I asked.

"I think I'm going to copy the Lord's Prayer onto some of that ivory-colored art paper of Mrs. Foster's. And then draw a border around the edge."

Mary Ruth's drawing was beautiful. I often watched her surround her paper with tiny delicate flowering vines and leaves. I almost asked her if she wouldn't make one for me to give to Grandma Martha, but it wouldn't be right.

"I don't know how to make anything," I said.

"We have to know," Violet said.

"Why don't you ask Mrs. Foster?" Mary Ruth said. "She always helps the little children make things to give their families."

At recess I asked Mrs. Foster if she had any ideas for gifts I could make.

"Well, I am having my younger students make picture frames from driftwood, shells, and pebbles they find on the beach. Then I will have them paint a picture to put inside." She showed me a sample of the project. It was very pretty the way she had small shells and smooth rocks glued to the wood.

But I could never paint a picture good enough to give to anyone. That was for little children or someone with talent, like Mary Ruth.

After school, with the little pocket money my father had given me, I went to the store to find a gift I could buy for Grandma Martha, Uncle Samuel, and Aunt Ivy. I asked Mary Ruth to go with me, because I didn't want to go alone. Tom Jonee made me uncomfortable. I didn't know if Henry told his father that I saw him start the fire, but I still didn't want to go by myself. So together, Mary Ruth and I crossed the street from the school.

The store looked like a house, but it sat further out on pilings than the other buildings. On the edge of the dock was a diesel pump where fishing boats could buy fuel. Tom Jonee watched out the window when villagers pumped their tanks full before coming in to pay him.

In the store Tom Jonee sat in his usual place behind a low counter. I never saw him anywhere else, never outside the store, never even working among the items for sale. He was always there, in that chair. Behind him was a wall of shelves that was Tahkeen's post office. When we came in he didn't look over and nod as usual but stared out at the dock, even though no boat was fueling.

Mary Ruth and I slowly walked up the two aisles, hoping some idea of a gift that I could afford would become obvious. Crackers, canned vegetables, lard, soap, brooms, and scrubbing powder lined the shelves, all simple basic things for hardworking people without much money to spend.

The air smelled dusty, as if the items had sat in the same place for years. I knew people bought much of what they needed here, but it felt more like a museum than a store. There was certainly nothing that looked like a gift.

When I glanced back at Tom Jonee, he placed a slim package from the mail shelf onto the counter. It was obviously put there for me to see. I walked toward it. Mary Ruth followed. Still he did not acknowledge us. I came close enough to see that it was addressed to me from Seattle.

"My pictures," I said to Mary Ruth. "They're here."

Tom Jonee stood up and leaned forward just as I took the envelope into my hands. His face was close to mine. I thought he and his son looked very much alike, a small square head with narrow eyes. Tom Jonee combed his hair straight back from his forehead like a black cloud hovering over a round hill. I could almost smell his breath and I stepped back, surprised.

"I heard what you told Foster about my son," he said. "I heard you said Henry started the fire in the old house."

His anger pushed at me. I looked over to Mary Ruth

for support, but she stood frozen in surprise. He saw me glance over to her and said, "Mary Ruth, go home. What I have to say is for her." His eyes seemed to be pounding out of his head and I backed away.

"I'm sorry, Clearie," Mary Ruth murmured. She ran out of the store.

"Please don't go," I begged. But she had fled.

As soon as the door shut behind Mary Ruth, Tom Jonee said, "You ugly white pig. People will not stop buying from Tom Jonee. You have no say here. You are trash. Even the Indian part of you is garbage."

I stepped back and bumped into a broom leaning against the shelves. It clattered against the wooden floor and everything in my stomach jumped hard into my throat.

"You better stay out of Tom Jonee's way," he said, tapping his chest. "Or you'll be sorry."

I put my hand up to my mouth, and my skin felt sticky and hot. I turned and ran out of the store.

I went along the beach to avoid meeting anyone. Tom Jonee thought he knew what I was like. He has heard something about my mother, I thought. He thinks I'm just like her. I ran all the way past Grandma Martha's, pushing my feet through the loose rocks of the beach. At the other end of the village, by the deserted houses, I crawled up the bank and slipped around the end of the tribal house to the trail. I left tears marking my path.

When I came to the stone wolf I threw my arms around its neck and hugged myself into the folds of cold stone. I wanted the chill against me. I was hot with fear and hurt. Pig, pig, ugly white pig. I hung on tight to the grinning animal as if it could keep me from sinking away into the dirt like rain. Pig, pig, ugly white pig. I kept hearing Tom Jonee's words. The remembered sound of his voice grew inside, bulging, until I felt I would burst.

Finally, exhaustion swept in and the tears slowed. I let go of my stone anchor and sat leaning against the base. As I calmed down, anger started replacing my embarrassment. I realized that Tom Jonee didn't know anything about me. He had known my mother when she lived in Tahkeen, but I'd only been here for six weeks. He couldn't possibly know what kind of a person I was. He said those horrible things trying to cover up for his son. It was the truth I told Reverend Foster, and I wasn't going to let Tom Jonee or his son scare me into lying. I took deep breaths and hoped I could clear my face of trouble.

After a few minutes I felt calmer. My eyes still stung from crying, but my fingers no longer trembled. I remembered the pictures and opened the envelope. There were pictures of Grandma Martha's house, the church, and the tribal house.

Then I turned over a snapshot that Mark had taken outside the church of Grandma Martha, Aunt Ivy, Uncle

Samuel, and me together. Gray people in the palm of my hand, as if all of us in the photo were also carved of stone like the creature behind me. I looked at our faces: mine in the middle staring straight at the camera, my grandmother, aunt, and great-uncle looking at me, their frozen gazes holding me cradled between them.

My hands seemed to grow warmer like thawing ice. As I held the pictures my determination to be frozen against my relatives was melted. Just looking at their faces made me think of every kind thing they had said to me or done for me since I came to Alaska.

Then I knew, this would be my gift to them, this picture of us together. I would make a frame, like the one Mrs. Foster showed me, to surround it just as they stood around me in the picture and held me in place.

I walked back to the beach. Working quickly before dark covered me, I began searching for bits of wood and shell. I filled my pockets before going home.

10
CALM PEACE
KAYEIL'

Good cheer blew into the village during Christmas week. Several days before Christmas Eve, I went with Grandma Martha and Aunt Ivy to the Fosters' where we filled bags with candy, little toys, and oranges for Santa to pass out to the smaller children.

In the school, we put up a tree that Reverend Foster and Uncle Samuel cut in the woods. I helped string popcorn and make paper chains to hang on the branches of the tree. For the top there was a star made out of heavy gold foil with tiny holes poked all over it. A lightbulb fit inside, and when plugged into the generator, it shone through the holes of the star.

I was glad to be busy. If I glanced toward the store, or caught a glimpse of a man that might be Tom or Henry

Jonee, fear and anger seared through my limbs. Every day I was scared Grandma Martha or Aunt Ivy would ask me to go to the store for them. I knew I never wanted to face the Jonees again.

The weather stayed clear and cold. Afternoons were often calm enough for me to take Uncle Samuel's boat out for a quick lap around the bay. I put on many layers of clothes and paddled fast in order to stay warm.

I was out on the bay when Hosket's troller came in with Mark on board, home for Christmas break. He yelled over to me, "Merry Christmas, Clearie." The sound of his voice skimmed across the water. "You look like you've been paddling all your life."

I happily waved my paddle in reply and headed for the beach. When I landed I saw Mark come trotting over the pebbles from the fuel dock where his father had tied up. I hooked the winch line onto the bolt on the bow of the canoe and started cranking. This pulled the heavy boat up the steep incline of the beach.

"Hey, that's quite a contraption." Mark said.

"Hi to you too," I said.

"When did Samuel rig this up?"

"Soon after you went back to school. I couldn't pull the boat far enough away from the water by myself so Uncle Samuel nailed the winch to the piling here by the house."

"It's a great idea," he said.

"He had to. One time I left the boat near the waterline and went to find Uncle Samuel to help me pull it up the beach. While I was gone, the tide came in and grabbed it. The canoe floated away."

"How far did it go?" Mark asked.

"Almost all the way to the mouth of the river. We had to borrow your father's canoe to go get it. Uncle Samuel kept mumbling about the Kushtarka gobbling it up."

Mark laughed. "I have to help my father take the boat out to anchor. I'll see you tomorrow night."

The next day was Christmas Eve. Grandma Martha fried doughnuts and baked white-sugar cookies that we would take to the celebration that night. Fish soup made from salmon, cod, and canned milk stayed warm on the edge of the stove.

As we were getting ready for church I noticed a package, wrapped in brown paper on the table. I quickly went and got the picture frame. I placed my small gift on the table beside the bigger bundle.

Grandma Martha said, "What is this?"

"It's for all of you," I said. "From me."

Grandma took the paper off and her eyes showed a soft gladness. "It is wonderful, Granddaughter."

"Hang it here next to the picture of our Jesus," Aunt Ivy said.

I felt a small pride grow in me. It was plain to see they really liked the gift, even Aunt Ivy.

Grandma pushed the larger package over to me. Inside the wrapping sat a thick sweater, knit from the same cream colored wool that Aunt Ivy used as a background in her weaving. It was similar to the ones the other kids in the village wore to school. This one had the Tlingit design of the eagle knitted into the back.

"This sweater is as warm as any coat," Grandma Martha said.

"It's wonderful," I pulled it on over my head. The sweater was big and soft, like wearing a blanket.

Uncle Samuel then took something from behind the cook stove. "I have made my great-niece a gift."

He put it on the floor in front of me. It was a wooden weaving frame like Aunt Ivy's. I saw them wait expectantly for my reaction. I ran my fingers over the smoothed joints where Uncle Samuel had carefully put the pieces together. It felt comfortable to my fingers.

Uncle Samuel's face was so hopeful. "Inside there," Uncle Samuel said pointing to where the weaving would be, "you fill the space with your life."

"I don't understand," I said.

"The *naaxein*, the traditional Tlingit blanket, it lives inside you. As you weave, your fingers draw out the story."

"Thank you, Uncle Samuel," I said. I wanted to hug him, but held back out of embarrassment. "Thank you, everyone." Both these gifts were given with so much thought and care. No one had ever done that for me before.

"The loom is only for if you want to learn. Someday," Aunt Ivy said. She looked to Grandma Martha uncertainly.

How many times I had walked past Aunt Ivy as she worked at her loom and admired her smooth movements. She was always happy when she was weaving. "I'd like to try," I said.

Grandma Martha brought her hands together in a clap of delight, but Aunt Ivy was more guarded. She said, "You tell me when you feel ready to start."

When it was time to go, Aunt Ivy wrapped the big soup pot in a heavy blanket to keep it warm. Grandma Martha lined two of her baskets with towels and piled the sweets into them like delicate birds in a nest. Uncle Samuel held the lantern, and we started off to the celebration.

Bouncing balls of light were coming out of all the houses and dancing toward the church. I could see the windows burning bright white with electric lights powered by the generator.

Inside, the church was hot and noisy. We placed the dishes of food we brought on the row of desks. Already some people were walking down the line filling their plates with canned vegetables, biscuits, and small chunks of fried fish, the same foods we ate almost every day. But there were also many treats in honor of the holiday. The smell of baked gingerbread almost overpowered the smell of fish. The thought of dessert made my mouth fill up until I had to swallow several times.

Mary Ruth was showing me her new gloves by the woodstove when the room became quiet. People parted; I saw Tom and Henry Jonee come in carrying a big tub between them. They set the heavy thing down where we could see it was filled with a yellow liquid. There was a slight feeling of discomfort among everyone, although some did greet the two men with a nod. It was as if everyone understood that this place was off-limits to the Jonees. I tried to push myself behind Mary Ruth and the chimney pipe so I wouldn't be seen. Mary Ruth squeezed my hand in understanding.

"I bring a gift for my neighbors," Tom Jonee said. "No one can say Tom Jonee is not a generous man."

I heard in his voice a hint of the anger he had showed me that day in his store. He knows he's not welcome here, I thought. I watched him poke at Henry's arm and motion toward the door with his head. They were leaving. I was so relieved. They turned to go and I peeked out from where I was. When they turned, Henry Jonee's eyes met mine and I froze. His stare hurt like a burn and I thought I saw him mouth silently the word "pig." I quickly looked down at my shoes until I was sure they had left.

Finally, Mary Ruth nudged me and said, “Henry’s the pig. Come on, there’s Mark and Violet. Let’s get in line with them.”

“What did Tom Jonee bring?” I asked Mary Ruth as we pushed through the crowd.

“Lemonade,” she said. “Every year he presents it to us as if it were liquid gold instead of the juice of lemons.” A lot of people were dipping cups into the tub as we passed, but it was poison to me. We picked up plates and stood by Mark and his sister.

“Hi,” Mark said. “This is always the best meal of the year.”

“Let’s start,” I said, trying to push any thought of Henry and Tom Jonee far away.

When we finished eating, the doors of the school were suddenly flung open and the familiar, “Ho, Ho, Ho, Merry Christmas,” swam through the room. There, coming in, was the smallest, skinniest Santa I had ever seen. His red suit hung on him like it was made for someone three times his size, and his beard was a piece of white sheet cut out in a semicircle. I looked at his face and recognized the shiny black eyes and shy expression of my great-uncle Samuel.

In the middle of the room he placed a burlap sack, filled with the treats I had helped to prepare. All the little ones moved in close, and Uncle Samuel gaily started handing them bags of goodies.

The rest of us were pushed back by the excitement. Mark stood over by his sister several feet away, while Mary Ruth and I crowded around one of the tables.

During the squeals and laughter of the children tearing open their treats, Uncle Samuel pressed a small square into my hands. It was wrapped in red paper and tied with twine. My name was printed on the top. I looked at Uncle Samuel, silently questioning him. He smiled and shrugged his shoulders.

"Who is that from?" Mary Ruth asked.

"It doesn't say." I tore off the paper. Inside lay a medallion carved out of cedar wood, in the shape of a feather. On the front, a flying eagle was etched in beautiful detail. At the top was a tiny hole with a black ribbon threaded through it so I could wear it around my neck.

"Who could have given it to me?"

"I noticed Violet is wearing one like it," Mary Ruth whispered.

I stared in surprise over to where Violet and Mark stood. Around Violet's neck was a similar carving. When I looked at them Mark put his hands in his pockets and turned away.

After everyone finished eating and the dishes were cleared away, Reverend Foster signaled it was time to start church.

Mark moved beside me while we pulled the long wooden church benches out into the room.

"Did you . . ." I started to ask, fingering the medallion.

He said, "I made one for Violet, and I thought maybe . . ." He paused and reddened. "Maybe you would like one too."

Before I could say anything else Reverend Foster switched off the generator and said we should take our seats. The service began in the soft silent light of the decorated tree and candles. We sang the hymns of Christmas with hushed voices, like my canoe swishing through the bay. Some of the children who had screamed with excitement a few minutes before now yawned and lay their heads on a lap next to them.

Standing up in front of us, Reverend Foster said, "Let us welcome this night of birth." And I understood, for the first time ever, what Christmas should be.

11 Evening Shadows

Chex'i

After Christmas, every day of vacation was fun. In the morning Mark stuck his head in the door to fetch Uncle Samuel, and they would go to work in the workshop. But after lunch Mark, Mary Ruth, Violet, and I would spend the afternoon together. One day we went sliding on wide boards, down the steep snowy hill behind the school. Another time we took turns with Mark's fishing pole, casting the line into the river from the bank.

On the Friday after New Year's Day, we went paddling in the Hoskets' large canoe. Working together, we tried to see how fast we could go. Then someone would miss a stroke, their paddle would collide with someone else's, and we would end up laughing while going in circles. I was so proud when it became clear that, after Mark, I was the best paddler, far better than Violet or Mary Ruth.

Eventually, we made our way down toward the mouth of the river. From there we could see streams of eagles fly away from their feeding areas on the river and disappear into the evergreens on the hillsides.

"Where are they going?" I asked.

"At night they rest together in the big trees," Mark said.

"Remember when we went hunting with Father up there?" Violet said to Mark. She pointed toward one of the narrow valleys that emptied itself into the river. Mark blushed.

"What happened?" Mary Ruth asked.

"We were walking under one of those trees, looking for a place to camp," Violet said.

"You don't need to tell this story," Mark said.

Violet laughed. "Just as we stopped we heard the soft sound of the eagles' voices. Mark looked up and from the branches above, splat, eagle doo all over his face."

I couldn't help giggling, but for Mark's sake I tried to hide it. "Eagles make the strangest sound," I said. "Not anything like I would expect from such a large bird."

"It sounds like a little whistle," Mary Ruth said.

"I think long ago the big eagle and the smaller hawk must have changed voices," Mark said. "Let's ask your uncle about it, Clearie."

Heading back toward the village we were quiet. It was a nice quiet. The long afternoons I had spent alone in my room before I came to Alaska suddenly felt as if they belonged to someone else. I wondered, Why did my mother hate this place?

When we came back into Tahkeen we saw the Jonees' troller set anchor. On the deck, Henry Jonee loaded several boxes into his motor skiff. As we passed, Henry stopped and stared at our boat. We were close enough that he could easily recognize us. The sudden tension made us feel damp. We stayed quiet so as not to embarrass Mary Ruth. Despite her father's promise in church not to drink, I guessed he would be among those waiting to buy from Henry Jonee.

Mark said, "There are going to be very low tides this weekend."

His comment distracted us. It was true. I had never seen so much beach in front of the village before. We landed the boat far out from the houses. Then the four of us started pulling hard to move the heavy canoe up to its resting spot in front of Hoskets. I thought to myself, at least Henry Jonee will have to sweat for his money tonight.

The job of securing the boat was made harder by the wet beach freezing into a solid sheet of ice. It took us a half an hour of pushing and slipping before we were able to drag the boat safely above the high-tide line.

"Come to our house and get warm," Violet invited.

A small crowd was gathering around where Henry Jonee landed. Mary Ruth glanced down the beach. "No, I must go home. My mother will want me."

I watched Mary Ruth hurry in the direction of her house. I didn't want the wonderful afternoon to end, and I knew Grandma Martha wouldn't mind if I stayed until dinnertime.

"We still have Christmas cookies left, don't we Violet?" Mark said.

"Yes, and we can make tea."

It was a half hour later, almost six, when I started for home. Mark said, "I'll take you."

As we got our coats and hats on, Mr. Hosket came in, "Mark, I need you to hold the light so I can finish changing the spark plugs on the boat."

"We saw Henry Jonee come in tonight," Mark said.

"I know," Mr. Hosket said. "Clearie, tell Samuel and Martha that tomorrow Reverend Foster wants as many people as possible at the church to talk about a buying trip to Sitka."

"You're going to try Clearie's idea?" Violet asked.

Suddenly, the room felt too hot. "It's not really my idea," I said. The thought of Tom Jonee's words was like someone holding their hand over my face. I couldn't breathe.

Mr. Hosket said, "I think we have to try something. Maybe if a few of us start, others will join."

I had to get out of there.

"You will tell your uncle?"

I nodded. "I can walk by myself," I said, wanting to be out the door.

Once outside, I felt better. The street was quiet. I was glad that Henry Jonee's customers seemed to have gone somewhere else to do their drinking. It never took long for Henry Jonee to sell every bottle he had.

By the time I reached my door I was out of breath. Even before saying hello, I said, "Uncle Samuel, Grandma Martha, Reverend Foster said he wants to meet at the church tomorrow to plan the boycott." Uncle Samuel frowned.

After dinner I couldn't relax; I paced around and around. Every time I sat down my nervousness started again, and I thought of the meeting the next day. I wondered if Tom Jonee would blame me. If he did, what would he say or do?

Several times I tried to read, but after a few words I just stared at the page. So I would get up and look out the windows, walk into my room, and then return again.

Aunt Ivy watched me from where she sat spinning pieces of white mountain goat hair into yarn. Finally, I sat down by the pile of wool where she worked. I had to tell someone, or I'd go crazy.

Grandma Martha was washing dishes and Uncle Samuel was dozing in his chair. Picking up a piece of wool in my hands, I held the scratchy softness of it between my flattened palms pressed together as if in prayer. I rubbed them back and forth, and the strands of hair began aligning themselves into a thread. Then I started rolling the fibers down my thigh, carefully stretching and twisting them into yarn as I had watched Aunt Ivy do so many times.

"Tom Jonee blames me for thinking of the boycott against him," I whispered to her so that Grandma Martha wouldn't hear.

"How do you know?" Aunt Ivy said.

The rocking motion of pushing the goat hair again and again down my leg filled up my arms and flooded into my chest. I could feel myself let go and breathe. It was the first easy breath I had since leaving Mark's house.

"He yelled at me in his store the last time I was there. He said he knew it was me who suggested fighting against him." Tears started up into my eyes. I wiped them away with my sleeve and willed myself not to cry.

Aunt Ivy pretended not to see I was upset. She took the piece of wool from my hands and showed me how to join it to the next piece to spin. Each motion she made was so automatic. When she handed it back to me, I took another section of hair from the pile and continued.

"Why would he blame you?" Aunt Ivy asked.

"Because I mentioned the idea to Mark. Buying things as a group was something my father said military people did. I didn't even think about it making someone mad or hating me for it."

"He can't hurt us," Aunt Ivy said.

"He thinks he can."

"Let us wait, Niece, and see what is decided tomorrow."

We worked on quietly. With every stroke of wool on my leg, I took a comfortable breath and felt myself relax. Aunt Ivy's fingers moved so quickly. Her yarn was smooth and even. Mine was thin in some places and fat and lumpy in others, but I didn't care. It felt good to watch my yarn grow longer. Grandma Martha came in and saw what I was doing. She smiled and touched my hair as she passed. The longer Aunt Ivy and I worked together, the better I felt.

The next day, just after lunch, we all met at the church. There were the Fosters, the Hoskets, Mr. Simons, and us.

Reverend Foster said, "If we go together and buy as much as possible in Sitka, Tom Jonee may stop Henry from making runs. And if we start, others will join us."

"What do we do?" Uncle Samuel asked.

"Make a list of goods you will need for the next two weeks and bring them to me tomorrow," Mr. Hosket said. "Monday, if the weather permits, Mark and I will go to Sitka and buy all the items on the list."

"Encourage others in the village, if you can. The more we have with us the better," Reverend Foster said.

"Put the amount of basic things like flour and sugar down as well," Mr. Hosket said. "If we buy a large amount of those items everyone needs and then divide it between us, we will save money."

"That money can be donated to a fund to pay for the fuel used in transporting everything," Reverend Foster said.

So, they were really going to do it. I knew it wouldn't take long for the Jonees to find out what was happening. What would I do if Henry or Tom Jonee tried to do something to me? Both those men were like ghosts, always hovering around, invading my days even when they were nowhere in sight.

12 Goose Moon

T'aawak Dis

I didn't expect to see Mark after the meeting. He and his father were spending the afternoon working on their boat, getting ready for the trip to Sitka on Monday. Back at home, Grandma Martha and Aunt Ivy sat down at the table to list things we needed. There was a feeling of excitement brought home from the meeting, a sense that we could control what was happening in our lives. For me, it made the decision to stop buying from Tom Jonee feel safer. While Grandma Martha wrote the list, Aunt Ivy worked her wool. I sat down beside her.

"There isn't much soap left," I said.

Grandma Martha wrote it down.

"We will need kerosene," Aunt Ivy said. She looked over at me, hesitating. Then she held out a handful of wool fibers. I took the bundle and fell into the rolling motion of turning it into yarn. Tea, sugar, flour, lard, canned corn, and milk finished our shopping list.

"Aunt Ivy?" I looked at the weaving frame Uncle Samuel had given me for Christmas.

"Yes?" she said.

I tried to push my question out of my mouth, but it was stuck.

"You have something to say, Niece?" Aunt Ivy asked.

"When can I learn how to weave?"

She didn't change expression. "Tomorrow we will start."

After dinner I kept looking over to the pile of yarn sitting next to my empty loom. I was still nervous about weaving. But after the meeting, for some reason, I felt more confident about trying. I guess I thought if we could change things in the village, maybe I could change things in my life. Besides, I could spin yarn now, and my mother never did.

When I was sitting down with a book to read, someone knocked at the door.

Uncle Samuel opened it to Mark. "Samuel, I was wondering if Clearie wanted to come down to the beach with Violet and me?" While Mark spoke to Uncle Samuel, he looked across the room at me.

"Now? This time of night?" I asked.

"The tide is low, and you must come see the ice," he explained.

I looked over to Grandma Martha to see if it was all right.

"We'll stay on the beach right in front of my house," Mark added.

"Go then, welcome *T'aawak dis* with your friends," she said.

I rushed to find my mittens and coat. When I was ready and heading for the door, I thought of my camera. It was a perfect night to take a picture of my first real friends. I grabbed the Brownie and hung the strap around my neck.

I stopped in the door and turned around. "I know that *dis* is moon, Grandma Martha, but what is *T'aawak*?"

"Goose," she said. "It is the goose moon."

"Violet is meeting us down at the beach below our house," Mark said as we walked through the cold. He added, "You know, I have lived here my whole life and I've never seen geese in January, ever."

I laughed. And laughing made me think of the times the four of us had spent together since Christmas. "Maybe we should stop and ask Mary Ruth if she wants to come."

"Okay."

Mark waited on the plank-walk while I climbed the three stairs up to the door. Mary Ruth's mother barely opened the door, only far enough to see out. She kept her face in the shadow.

"What do you want?" she asked.

"We're going to the beach, Mark, Violet, and I. I wondered if Mary Ruth could come?"

"No. It's not a good time."

Now my eyes were used to the darkness, and I could see that Irtha was disheveled and she was crying. And then I heard Mary Ruth's father yell her name, and she slammed the door.

"What was happening?" Mark asked.

"James," I said. I saw Mark understood. "Do you think we should tell your father or Reverend Foster?"

"No, I'm sick of James and his drinking," Mark said.

But I felt bad that I hadn't spoken with Mary Ruth, at least to make sure she was all right. I knew that if things had been just slightly different, it could have been me in a house with my drunk mother.

"It's not the first time James has made things hard for them. There's nothing we can do. Come on, hurry," Mark said. He ran the last few yards to the beach in front of his house. He stopped for a moment and shouted, "Violet, I've got Clearie." Then Mark sprinted out onto the beach as fast as he could. He hit the sheet of ice at the high-tide line, whooping as he leaped. I stood in amazement. Everywhere he landed the ice lit up under his feet like the flashbulb of my camera. Mark slid across the ice, leaving a trail of light streaks slashing.

I realized that the light was caused by the same phosphorescence that had been in the bay in November. It was back, and some of it had become frozen in the ice that formed at low tide.

Violet came up beside me. I snapped a picture of Mark before putting my camera down on a log, where it would be safe. Then we looked at each other and went screaming out to join Mark.

The three of us ran and slid, making patterns of glowing lights like stars and moons beneath our feet until we were sweating and out of breath. Finally we all flung ourselves down on logs, laughing and panting.

"Let's build a fire," Mark said. "Then we can slide some more." We gathered pieces of wood and placed them inside a ring of stones.

Comfortably watching the fire, we grew quiet. I started to think about Mary Ruth again and wondered what was happening at her house. "I wish Mary Ruth were here."

"We should have asked her to join us," Violet said.

Mark threw a small stick into the flames. "James is drinking."

"Then I should go tell Father," Violet started to stand as if she would leave that instant.

"What's he going to do?" Mark said. "If the stupid fool chooses to drink himself to death, no one can stop him."

"But what about Mary Ruth, Irtha, and Douglas?

They shouldn't have to suffer," Violet slowly sat down again.

"Irtha should kick him out," Mark said. "Maybe then he would shape up."

Through Mark and Violet's whole conversation I nervously twisted my hands together. "I think I know what they are going through."

Mark and Violet looked surprised at my tone of voice.

My throat closed tight. "My mother," I said. They waited for me to continue, but it was too hard. It seemed as though every muscle in my body had seized up to keep my secret imprisoned inside.

Finally, through my shaking body I forced the words out. "Since coming to Tahkeen, I've remembered that my mother drank and couldn't stop."

"I'm sorry," Violet said. "We didn't know." Violet moved close to me on the log. Staring into the flames Mark sat quietly.

The whole time we talked about Mary Ruth's father, I saw my mother at the table again. I was still pulling on her arm, crying, "Please, Mama, please." I remembered that she was in her nightgown and had thrown up all over herself. I kept saying, "Get up, get up." But she didn't move.

It was horrible to admit to myself that my memory was real. My fingers hurt from holding them in a tight fist. My father never told me about her, but I knew. He must have tried to protect me by hiding the truth.

I could see him in my mind that horrible night when he came home and found me crying over my mother where she had passed out. He silently placed her on the couch and then lifted me up onto his shoulders and carried me out the door. I don't remember what we did, but I remember my fingers touching tears on his face where I clung to him. What misery my father must have suffered when my mother drank.

"What happened to your mother?" Mark asked. He was looking at me intently, almost like he could see what I was remembering.

"I don't know," I said, forcing myself to open my hands. There were little dents left in my palms where my fingernails dug into the skin.

"You never knew where she went?" he asked.

"One day I came home from kindergarten and instead of my mother being there, a neighbor lady was waiting for me. She told me I was to come to her house until my father came home."

"Your mother didn't even say good-bye to you?" Violet asked.

"I don't remember," I said. "And my father wouldn't talk about her. He said I wasn't to, either."

"I think Irtha would be better off if James left like your mother did," Mark said. "I don't know how they can stand him."

Now I couldn't stop the tears from running. "Since I was five years old I believed that if I had been a good girl, you know, done everything my parents told me to, my mother wouldn't have left. I think Irtha and Mary Ruth are like that, too. They think if they are good enough to James, he'll stop drinking."

"Do you still feel it's your fault your mother ran away?" Violet asked.

Did I? I hadn't ever put my feelings into words before, but so much more made sense to me now. "I don't think so," I said. "Aunt Ivy and Grandma Martha both said that she was unhappy even before I was born."

When I said this to Violet I felt clean and scoured out. Old feelings now took on new meaning. Like my father's anger — I saw it was a wall he put up so nobody could see in to where he was hurting, not even me. But he should have told me, helped me to understand.

Mark and Violet didn't ask any more questions. Soon the fire burned down to a pile of hot coals, and Mrs. Hosket yelled down from the doorway that it was time to come in. We put the fire out, and I hung my camera around my neck.

Mark started to walk me home. He carried the lantern in his raised arm. Our light crawled across the front of the store building, and there was Henry Jonee, leaning against the wall, smoking. We tried to pass without saying anything to him. Mark took my arm. Being connected to him made me feel safe and strong.

Henry Jonee watched us until we were almost past. "I heard about your meeting this morning," he said.

Mark stopped. "So?"

"I'm talking to her," Henry said.

"It's not my meeting," I said. I started to shake. I moved out of the light so Henry wouldn't see the fear in my face.

"My father says you can't stop us. And we can make you wish you never came here," he said.

"Leave me alone," I said. I could feel the uncertainty in my own voice.

"Let's go, Clearie," Mark said. "Don't listen to him."

We hurried away, but Henry called after us, "You're going to be sorry." I heard the door of the store slam as Henry Jonee went in.

I gasped for breath.

"Don't let that creep upset you," Mark said.

"He hates me," I said.

"Henry Jonee hates everybody. And you stood up to him. That frightens him."

We stopped by my door and Mark held the light up and looked at me. "Please don't be upset," he said.

"He hates me not just because I told on him, but because I'm part white."

"Almost everyone here is part something. He's probably mad because you fit in more than he does. Let's forget it, okay? I'll see you tomorrow."

Mark's words made me feel better.

It was dark inside. Grandma Martha, Aunt Ivy, and Uncle Samuel were already asleep. I felt my way over to my room in the blackness. As I came to the window by my bed, I noticed a small light out on the bay where the fishing boats were anchored. I wondered who was working on their boat at this time of night?

The light grew and I realized it was coming from the wheel house on Uncle Samuel's troller. My stomach jumped to my throat. Fire!

13 Devil Fish

Naakw

I stood there, staring at the tiny fire growing spark by spark. Without moving, I kept telling myself, Do something; wake everybody up. At last I forced myself to yell, "Uncle Samuel!" My muscles followed my words, and I ran into the main room.

"The boat's on fire!" I screamed, pointing in the direction of the water.

Uncle Samuel pushed himself up from sleep and looked out the window. Grandma Martha and Aunt Ivy came rushing down the stairs.

"What is it? What is wrong?" Grandma Martha asked.

Without answering Uncle Samuel rushed to the door.

"Samuel!" Grandma Martha called.

"His boat, it's burning," I cried.

Grandma Martha and Aunt Ivy came to the window.

"Dear God," Grandma Martha murmured.

"I'll go for help," Aunt Ivy said.

As she slipped into her coat I heard the canoe winch under the house unwind. I ran outside. I still had my coat on from the beach, and my camera banged on its strap against my chest. Uncle Samuel was pulling the canoe across the icy beach. I ran out and started pushing from behind. He was barefoot and dressed only in his long underwear.

"Niece, go back."

"I can help you," I said. We hit the water, jumped in, and each grabbed a paddle. A hard breeze skimmed the surface of the water. Short, choppy waves slapped against the boat and were difficult to push through. I noticed, though, that even in his panic, every stroke Uncle Samuel took was sure and even. He made the canoe come alive, like a killer whale or a seal sliding through the sea. I heard the bell at the schoolhouse announce the emergency.

We weren't very far out when I caught a glimpse of another boat tied up against Uncle Samuel's troller. Thank goodness, I thought, there's someone already there, trying to put out the fire. In less than five minutes, we pulled alongside the boat. The troller had swung around on its anchor, so that the other boat was facing away from us. Uncle Samuel grabbed a bailing bucket from the bottom of the canoe and leapt onto the deck of his boat. He leaned over the side, scooping up water to throw on the flames that came from inside the pilot-house.

I tied the canoe's bowline to the stern of the thirty-foot troller, all the while trying to see who had arrived before us to help. Grabbing the edge of the troller to steady myself, I jumped aboard.

Then, in the glare, I glimpsed a dark outline climbing into the other boat. The person was leaving. I ran over. With the light behind me I saw it was Henry Jonee.

"What are you doing? Stop!" I grabbed his arm and tried to pull him back into the troller. He swung his other arm at me. The empty gas can he was holding in that hand hit against me with a tinny echo. I jumped out of the way, and he moved both legs over the edge, ready to slide into his skiff.

Suddenly, my camera banged against my chest and I knew what to do. Quickly aiming, I snapped a picture of Henry Jonee, gas can in hand, perched on the rail of Uncle Samuel's boat. The flash lit his face and he flung an arm in front of his head. This time I would have proof that Henry Jonee started the fire.

"Hey!" he shouted. He tossed the can into the water and started back into the boat after me. I moved as far back to the stern as I could. Henry Jonee, framed by the hot glare of the fire, looked like a black monster coming closer and closer. My mouth filled with a terrible taste and I realized I was about to vomit. I swallowed and the fear was hot going down my throat. I tried to scream for Uncle Samuel, but no words could come out. And all of Uncle Samuel's attention was on frantically throwing buckets of water on the flames.

Henry reached out a hand that smelled like gasoline and clenched the hair at the back of my head. He pulled me close to him, and the smell of whiskey and smoke joined with the gasoline scent.

"Give me the camera," he said. His other hand grabbed the leather strap and jerked on it. It cut into the skin on my neck but didn't break.

"Stop it! Stop it!" I pushed with both hands against him and then I kicked him as hard as I could on the leg. He yelled and stepped back for a second.

He glared and swung his fist. I saw the hand coming in slow motion. I couldn't do anything to stop it. I imagined what the pain was going to feel like. But suddenly a jolt hit the boat as another canoe came alongside. With the boat rocking, the fist heading for my face changed direction and rose into the smoky air. I had to take a step to the side with one leg and brace myself. But Henry Jonee was unable to keep his balance when the Hoskets' canoe bumped against the hull of our troller.

Henry's feet slipped from underneath him and he fell. In that second, while he lay confused on the deck, I reached down through the dark, feeling around desperately for anything I could use against him. I grabbed something wooden. He was sitting up. It fit well in my hand. He rose to one knee and drew himself up. I lifted my weapon, still not knowing what it was. When he lunged for me I swung, like I was swinging a baseball bat. It hit him just below his shoulder, flinging him to one side of the boat. The force of the blow threw me in the other direction. I landed in the back deck corner just in time to look up and see Henry tip over the edge of the rail and into the water. On the other side of the boat, Mark and his father climbed aboard.

I crawled over to see what happened to Henry Jonee, keeping my fish club weapon with me just in case he tried to climb back aboard. I raised my face to peer into the water and saw him slowly pulling himself into his skiff. He untied the line and pushed away from us, drifting off without trying to start the outboard.

It was then I began to notice the other battle being fought. Uncle Samuel already looked tired, but Mark, his father, Reverend Foster, and two other men from the village were starting to drench the cockpit with water.

I put my camera down in the back of the boat and looked for another bucket.

"Over there, over there!" Uncle Samuel yelled. I looked to where he was pointing.

Another canoe landed against the side of the boat and several other men from the village went right to work putting out the fire. The fishing boat was surrounded now with narrow canoes jutting out like roots from a tree.

"Make fire lines, from either side of the boat," Mr. Hosket shouted. We fell into four lines. In mine I was on the outside, the person who leaned over the rail to fill the pail. I passed the water to Reverend Foster and he passed it on to Mark, who threw it on the fire. Uncle Samuel, the last person on our side, carried the empty buckets back to me. I forced myself to work even though I still trembled from my fight with Henry Jonee.

Each time I leaned over the shiny black surface of the water a sudden fear of something grabbing from the deep almost stopped me. I thought I would see Henry Jonee's face peering up at me from just under the water like the *Naakw,* the spiny devil fish Uncle Samuel told me about. Then I thought of Aunt Ivy, and her voice filled my mind. "Be strong," I heard her say, and I pushed my fears away.

Within a few minutes I could see the fire start to die. The flames became smaller, shrinking back into the center of the pilothouse. Where the flames had eaten at the sides of the cabin, the wood was left black and charred. There was more smoke than air. It felt oily in my lungs, like breathing diesel fuel. With every breath I coughed.

My arms and back ached. I was soaking wet from the water sloshing over the top of the pails and onto me. When I dipped my bucket into the cold sea for almost the last time, I looked back across the bay to the village. I knew that Grandma Martha and Aunt Ivy were waiting helplessly on the beach, afraid and worried, the knot of their support broken by the stretch of water they had no way to cross. I wished Aunt Ivy were there, so she could see how well I did.

Uncle Samuel stopped working when he saw that the fire was beaten and his boat would be saved. He bent down, resting his hands on his thighs, breathing hard and swaying slightly back and forth.

Moving around on the boat deck was becoming difficult because the water we splashed across the planking was freezing into ice. I carefully went over to him and said, "Uncle Samuel, sit down and rest." I wanted so much to wrap him up in a blanket of concern, but he didn't respond. Suddenly I heard a growl start to grow from far inside him. It came rushing out as a scream of anger, and he swung his empty bucket up over his head to smash it against the boat railing. As he did, the boat heaved to one side on a sudden wave. His feet gave way on the ice, and his tired body began to follow the slamming bucket almost like he was being pulled by a rope. Uncle Samuel's thigh fell against the rail and he went over.

Arms grabbed air as several men tried to stop his fall. Then all of us leaned over the edge to see where he lay, crumbled and jagged across the tops of the tethered canoes.

14

TEARS

DU WAX AHEENI

Mr. Hosket and Reverend Foster lifted Uncle Samuel carefully into the Hoskets' canoe. They removed their coats and placed them over him. A warmer wind was moving in from the south. It brought huge, wet snowflakes that fell so thickly it was hard to see the shore.

"He's barefoot!" Reverend Foster exclaimed.

"I think his leg is broken," Mr. Hosket said. "It looks crooked."

I carefully placed my camera into the bottom of my canoe and climbed in. Mark and I paddled behind the boat carrying Uncle Samuel across the bay. The tide was almost high when the bows of the two boats glided side by side against the gravel beach.

Grandma Martha came rushing over crying, "Samuel, what is wrong? Samuel!"

"He fell overboard. We aren't sure how he is," Mr. Hosket said. "But Martha, we need to get him inside and dry."

Aunt Ivy stood by Grandma Martha and held her arm. "Come," she said and led the procession up between the houses. The whole village had gathered on the beach during the fire. Now they fell in with us as we went to the house. "Put Uncle Samuel there," Aunt Ivy pointed to his cot by the cookstove.

Mr. Hosket quickly started to pull off the wet clothes and cover him with a stack of blankets. "That left leg must be broken," he whispered. "Is there frostbite?"

"I don't know if his toes are frozen. They haven't turned black, but I just can't tell," Reverend Foster said. They wrapped his feet in a warm towel. "There is something else wrong. Look at him struggling to breathe."

I held the kerosene light so they could see while Aunt Ivy collected dry things to put on him. Lying on the cot, Uncle Samuel looked tiny and old. His breath was loud and wheezing.

Grandma Martha sat apart, watching from the table. She held her hands tightly together shaking her head. "He is my only brother. Our whole lives we have lived together." Irtha comforted her.

Some of the men who had helped put out the fire stood around the living room. The others gathered outside the house, talking in quiet voices. They seemed to be trying to share in our problem so the burden would be lessened by everyone taking a piece of it to hold.

"We need to get him to the hospital," Reverend Foster said. "I don't think it can wait until morning, but it's a risk with this wind."

"Mark," his father told him, "get the boat ready. We can leave in thirty minutes."

"It must be blowing thirty, forty knots outside the bay," Reverend Foster said.

Reverend Foster and Mr. Hosket stood staring down at Uncle Samuel. I thought they were waiting for a solution or a sign to rise up out of his shriveled body, like steam from a kettle.

"We must do something," Aunt Ivy said. She held a cup of tea and knelt down beside Uncle Samuel. His eyes were open, but he looked around like he didn't know where he was. When Aunt Ivy tried to spoon some of the tea into his mouth, it just dribbled down the sloping side of his face.

"What do you want to say, Uncle?" Aunt Ivy leaned in close.

Uncle Samuel rocked his head back and forth, and with a half moan, half whine whispered through shredded breath.

"Ivy is right," Mr. Hosket said. "We must go as soon as possible. It could mean Samuel's life if we wait. We've gone in worse conditions."

"We'll get what we need for the trip," Aunt Ivy said. "Mother." She leaned down close to speak into Grandma Martha's ear. I could hear her try to steady her voice and sound determined. "Uncle Samuel will need us there with him." Her words acted like an alarm clock for Grandma Martha. She stopped wringing her hands and stood up while reason flooded through her.

"Aunt Ivy, what should I do?" I asked.

For just a second she looked at me as if she were trying to remember who I was. Mrs. Foster came and put her hands on my arms from behind.

"Don't worry, Ivy," she said. "Clearie can come and stay with us."

"Will that be all right, Niece?" Aunt Ivy asked.

I nodded. But really I wanted desperately to go with them so I would know if Uncle Samuel was going to be all right. Silently, I began to help Grandma Martha get ready.

When we carried Uncle Samuel to the dock, the snow had turned to rain, blowing in sideways on gusts of cold wind. We laid Uncle Samuel on a pallet of blankets inside the little cabin on the Hoskets' boat. Aunt Ivy and Grandma Martha crouched on either side of him to make sure he stayed covered and warm. Over the top of them they stretched a rubber tarp to keep him dry. As I stood on the dock, Grandma Martha reached out a hand and patted his head saying, "I am here, Brother. I am with you."

The boat disappeared into the darkness.

"Let's go get what you will need for the night," Mrs. Foster said. "Then we'll make cocoa."

The next five days passed very slowly while I waited to hear word from Sitka. I tried to think of things to keep me busy. I helped Mrs. Foster with school and spun all the goat hair Aunt Ivy had into yarn for her. Spinning without Aunt Ivy felt empty, though, even when I brought the goat hair back to the Fosters' to spin in the evenings.

Mrs. Foster sat down and watched me spin one evening.

"Ivy will be happy to see all you have done for her," she said.

After the boat fire, Henry wasn't seen anywhere in the village. His motor skiff was gone from the bay. Tom Jonee went to see Reverend Foster the very next day. That night during supper the Reverend told us, "Tom Jonee promised me there would be no more trouble, no more runs."

"That is good news," Mrs. Foster said.

Finally, on Wednesday, a letter came from Aunt Ivy. I read it aloud to Reverend and Mrs. Foster:

Dear Niece,

Samuel is resting in the hospital. He suffers with a broken leg and three cracked ribs. The doctor says he must remain for several weeks.

We are staying with your grandmother's cousin, Sophie. The trip and the worry were hard on your grandmother, but she is strong now that she is settled.

I reported the boat burning to the sheriff's office here in Sitka.

I will write when I have more news.

Aunt Ivy

Aunt Ivy's letter, simple as it was, made me feel so lonely for her, Grandma Martha, and Uncle Samuel. It was a new feeling that hung on me like a sack of stones flung over my shoulders. I never missed my father like that. It made me sad to realize this, but also a funny kind of gladness that I knew, now, what it was like to have people to really care about.

When it left, the same mail packet that brought Aunt Ivy's letter carried my film to Seattle for developing. I asked Mrs. Foster to put her name on the film and send it for me. I wasn't going to take any chances that the postmaster, Tom Jonee, would lose my pictures. This time, I was determined to have proof of what Henry Jonee did.

Uncle Samuel stayed in the hospital for three weeks. It

was a joy to watch him sitting on the deck of the mailboat when he, Grandma Martha, and Aunt Ivy came back to Tahkeen. I saw Aunt Ivy point to Uncle Samuel's troller with the blackened pilothouse. When their boat scraped the edge of the pilings they were still talking about it.

"The hull looks fine," Aunt Ivy said. "But we must repair the cabin quickly." She looked at me. "Fishing will soon begin."

I smiled back at her, filled with pleasure that she included me in her plans.

Reverend and Mrs. Foster helped carry things while Uncle Samuel slowly hobbled along the boardwalk on his crutches.

"Uncle Samuel should have my room," I suggested when we came inside. "So he'll have privacy and quiet to rest."

"No," Aunt Ivy said. "He will stay where he has always slept. There, he is near us and can see and hear everything that goes on. We are not too noisy for him." When Aunt Ivy said this I noticed how different she sounded. It was almost as if in the past three weeks she had become the parent to Uncle Samuel and Grandma Martha. Both Uncle Samuel and Grandma Martha nodded in agreement with Aunt Ivy.

Once Uncle Samuel was comfortable, Mrs. Foster and I filled them in on the news of the village. We told them of Henry Jonee leaving and how Tom Jonee had spoken to Reverend Foster.

"Tom Jonee even said hello to me," I said.

"What about the store?" Grandma Martha asked.

"Since Henry is gone and no whiskey is coming in," Mrs. Foster said, "we felt there wasn't any reason to go ahead with the boycott."

"It is a blessing to know our nights will be peaceful again," Grandma Martha said.

"There is one sad thing," Mrs. Foster said. "James has left Tahkeen, too."

"It was almost two weeks ago," I said. "He left without any word. Mary Ruth said her mother hasn't stopped crying."

"Poor Irtha," Grandma Martha said. "I must visit with her as soon as possible."

"Irtha doesn't want to say it, but James was in a terrible state after Henry Jonee left and the village has been dry," Mrs. Foster said.

It was the next week when Mrs. Foster gave Aunt Ivy the packet of pictures she picked up from the store.

As soon as Aunt Ivy placed it in my hands, I tore the envelope open and sifted through the pictures. "Here it is, Henry Jonee caught in the act. He's on Uncle Samuel's boat. Look, you can see the gas can in his hand." I handed Aunt Ivy the picture.

"Henry is definitely recognizable and the gas can, but

Clearie, how would anyone know it's Uncle Samuel's boat? I can't even tell it is a boat," Aunt Ivy said.

"I know it was Uncle Samuel's boat!"

"Yes, but he could be anywhere, on a gate or wall."

"I was there!" I said.

"He will deny it," Aunt Ivy said, handing me back the picture. She put her hand on my shoulder and added, "You were strong in your efforts."

I knew she was right. The proof I was so excited about and had waited for was nothing. I jammed the photo under a stack of books on the shelf in my room.

15 After Winter

Taakw It

After school and on weekends, all through March, I helped Aunt Ivy repair the troller. With Uncle Samuel, we made a list of supplies we needed. Aunt Ivy carefully checked how much wood and nails would cost against how much money was left from fishing last year. She showed Uncle Samuel.

"It will be enough," he said. "If we are careful."

"We still have to eat," Aunt Ivy said.

"We will use more of what the land gives us for free," he said.

"Yuck, more fish," I said.

"Good stuff," Uncle Samuel and Grandma Martha said together.

Through several late evenings Aunt Ivy and Uncle

Samuel discussed plans to rebuild the fishing boat's cabin. In his delicate handwriting, Uncle Samuel sketched a picture and labeled each step of the construction.

At high tide on the day our lumber order arrived, Aunt Ivy and I both held our breath and started the troller's engine. Slowly, we brought the boat into the gas dock to load the stack of boards. Aunt Ivy stood at the wheel while I perched on the bow with the line in my hand.

Back at anchor, we framed in the new pilothouse. That was like making the outline of a picture before coloring it in.

"Stop a minute, let me take a picture of you before we continue," I said to Aunt Ivy. "I want a picture of each stage of the work."

"Then I will take your picture," Aunt Ivy said. "You can send it to your father and he will know what a fine, strong girl you are becoming."

I was so happy when I heard Aunt Ivy's praise. I do feel stronger, I thought, and capable. There were so many things I had learned: paddling, fishing, spinning, and now carpentry. I looked down at my hands. They were hard and callused, so different from when I came to Alaska.

How many times my father had asked, "Can't you do anything right?" Then the image of him — sad, tired, his head cradled in his arm — came to mind, and I felt sorry for him. It felt so good for me to be honest and open with Aunt Ivy, Grandma Martha, and Uncle Samuel. My father had never shared his problems with me or anyone. He left them inside to boil and burn.

"I don't think my father would believe it, even if you told him," I said.

Aunt Ivy looked at me for a long moment and then she almost whispered, "Then you must believe for him." She pointed to my head like the night of the house fire and said, "Up here.

"My whole life I have been told that the things I wanted to do, such as fishing and fighting fires, were not for women," Aunt Ivy continued. "I have to always remind myself I can do it. Otherwise, I start to believe they are right."

I took a deep breath and asked, "Do you still think I'm like my mother?"

I saw tears start in Aunt Ivy's eyes. "No," she said. "Clearie, I'm sorry if I ever made you think that. I tried to love Dora so hard. But whatever I did for her, she just spit back at me. I have been angry at her for a long time."

"Why was she so unhappy?" I asked.

"I don't know," Aunt Ivy said. "But she always was. Dora started drinking when she was just a year or two older than you are. After that she was an empty shell."

"I don't want that to happen to me," I said.

"I believe right now you are growing deep roots and strong branches that can stand in any storm, Niece. Just remember strength comes from inside you."

"I'll try," I said.

"Let's remind each other now and then," Aunt Ivy said.

The fresh yellow wood we hammered into place made the growing pilothouse stand out like a glaring reflection from the other boats lined across the bay. Each night after working on the boat, we would stop on the beach and look back at the progress we had made.

"I never knew I could build anything," Aunt Ivy said one evening while we stood gazing out at the boat. "It was a mystery how a house or building went together. But really, it's so simple."

"You've made it better than it was by adding the two layers of tar paper in the walls," I said. "Think how warm it'll be."

That night, after thinking about everything Aunt Ivy said, I wrote to my father. I wanted him to see how much I had changed since coming to Alaska. But to simply say to him that I was growing wouldn't work. Then I remembered what Grandma Martha had said — to show him what I saw around me. It was my hope that by telling him what was now important to me, he would see me. In my letter, I told him about Uncle Samuel's injury and about helping Aunt Ivy repair the boat. Then I said:

It is March twenty-ninth today, exactly five months since I arrived in Alaska. When I first came all I saw and felt was the wet: the sea, the rain, the tides. Now when I get up in the morning, it is the wind I look for. Wind holds Tahkeen and moves us all around in it. Seals in the waves and eagles in the air use the breezes to shape their day, as do all of us here. Where to fish, what chores to do, what sights we see, are decided by the wind. It is a wonderful feeling. But I know my words by themselves can't show you what it's like, so here are some of the pictures I have taken with the camera you sent me. I want you to understand.

Your daughter,
Clearie

Aunt Ivy talked with Reverend Foster about fishing and then asked many more questions of Uncle Samuel. She filled a school notebook with instructions on everything from weather and map reading to bait and fishhooks.

"Soon, Niece," she said, "we must begin to practice running the boat and fishing in the bay. And then, when it is time for Uncle Samuel to be examined again in Sitka, we will take him ourselves."

Grandma Martha cared for Uncle Samuel every day. She helped him dress and move around. It was difficult for him to learn to use the crutches. He often grew tired and frustrated, trying to complete tasks that before his accident he didn't even have to think about. One evening, when Grandma Martha had helped him bathe and was getting him into his pajamas, he became agitated and pushed at her arms.

"Samuel, I cannot help you when you act this way. Be still now," she said.

Then in frustration he complained, "I am like a child, not a man."

"Everyday I see you grow stronger," Grandma Martha said. "You will not need my help for long. And I feel I am finally able to repay you for all the years you have taken care of me."

"A man should," he said.

"I was just a girl when Lester died. You gave up having a wife of your own to stay with me. Now I can show you I am grateful."

Grandma Martha's words only seemed to make Uncle Samuel more angry. The more upset he became, the more it looked like his cracked ribs hurt, making it difficult to breathe or speak. His good leg stamped the floor and he lashed at her with his arm when she came near.

Grandma Martha held her hands out, pleading, "I only want to help."

Then I thought it was the time to try an idea I had been thinking about since Uncle Samuel was in the hospital. Secretly, I had been practicing some of the stories that he told me before the accident. I was scared I would get the story confused or wrong and end up looking stupid. But I looked at my changed hands and reminded myself of what Aunt Ivy had said on the boat.

"Uncle Samuel," I said. "I'm going to tell the story of how Raven became black. Will you listen?" He stopped and focused his eyes on me. "I want you to see if I have it right."

Almost immediately he was more himself, and I could see I had captured his curiosity. Grandma Martha backed away and went to fill the kettle. She was still very upset. I hoped my idea would work out.

When he was ready, I sat down on the wood floor next to his cot and leaned my back against it. He relaxed against a stack of pillows with his cast propped up in front on a chair.

"Long ago, in the myth time, Raven was not black, as he is today, but white like clouds and ice," I said. I looked up at him and he nodded. "Then, Raven shared the world with several other great beings. The most powerful of these was Ganook, the sitting one.

"Once Raven and Ganook had a canoe race to see who was the stronger. Ganook wanted to show Raven he was better, so he took off his special hat and made a thick fog come out of it that covered the entire sea. This fog was so heavy that Raven could not see the edge of the boat where he held his paddle.

"Ganook quickly went ahead, leaving Raven lost.

Raven became frightened and yelled out, 'Ganook, where are you?' But Ganook stayed quiet. Raven was confused and paddled his boat around and around in circles just like lost people do. All the time Raven kept begging Ganook to show himself and make the fog go away. Finally, Ganook returned.

"'What's the matter? Why are you crying?' he asked.

"Raven said, 'You've won. You're much stronger and more powerful than I am.'

"When Raven said this, Ganook put his hat back on his head and the fog disappeared.

"After the race Ganook invited Raven to his island of Deikee Noow. There, they ate salmon and drank fresh-water from Ganook's special well. Raven had never tasted fresh-water before, because at that time, there was only seawater in the world. And Ganook protected his precious well by covering it with a heavy flat rock.

"Raven loved the taste of the clear, cold water and wanted more, but he was afraid to ask because Ganook had proven he was more powerful than Raven. After the meal Raven and Ganook told each other stories until at last Ganook fell asleep on top of the well lid.

"When he was sound asleep Raven found some dog doo and placed it under the sleeping Ganook. Then he shouted, 'Ganook, wake up! Look what you've done.' Ganook saw the brown pile. Thinking that he had messed himself, he ran to the beach to wash.

"With Ganook gone, Raven worked fast. He ran to the well and lifted the heavy lid and drank some water. Then he filled his mouth with water and started to fly up through the smoke hole of Ganook's house. But Ganook came in and caught Raven by the tip of his white talon. Ganook pulled him back into the lodge and held Raven over the fire as punishment for having tricked him. The smoke from the fire turned Raven's feathers and skin black. Raven pleaded and cried until finally Ganook took pity on him and let him go.

"Raven then flew away towards his home on the Nass River. As he flew, tiny drops of the freshwater he stole leaked from his beak and fell to earth. Wherever the drops of water landed, lakes, rivers, and springs appeared on the land."

As the story ended I watched Uncle Samuel laugh and relax. He reached out his arm and touched my cheek. Just then Grandma Martha placed a cup of tea into his hand and his eyes shined up to her.

"Oh Granddaughter, that is a wonderful gift you have given. Thank you," she said.

"I hoped Uncle Samuel would like it."

"Anytime," Uncle Samuel said, smiling.

I started to collect more Tlingit stories to tell Uncle Samuel. I asked anyone who would take the time to tell me one, even Reverend Foster. When I asked him, he laughed and rubbed his belly. "I never thought anyone would ask a fat old white man for Indian stories," he said. But he knew several about Owl and Eagle and, of course, the trickster, Raven.

"You should write these stories down, Clearie," Reverend Foster said. "We could use them in the school. I bet there isn't one pupil who knows the old legends. They could easily be lost forever."

"Like a book of some kind?" I asked.

"Yes. Feel free to use Mrs. Foster's typewriter," Reverend Foster said.

The stories began to feel like Uncle Samuel's carving or Aunt Ivy's *naaxein* to me, something I could leave behind when I left Alaska.

But I didn't want to leave Tahkeen. I didn't want to leave story collecting, spinning, and paddling on the bay. And I didn't want to leave my family here. Besides, now I was needed. I really could help Grandma Martha, Uncle Samuel, and Aunt Ivy, I had proved it! And through everything we had become tangled together in a way that couldn't just be torn apart. To go back to that lonely life of before was a thought that hurt.

16

The Little Dipper

Yaxte

That very evening I sat at the table peeling carrots with Grandma Martha. Uncle Samuel was in his regular chair with his leg propped up on a wooden box. Aunt Ivy was weaving.

"Granddaughter, your hand moves as slow as the glacier ice. Where is your head tonight?" Grandma Martha asked.

"I just realized how fast time is going by. Tomorrow is April third," I said.

"What made you think of this?" she asked.

"I don't want to have to go back," I said very quietly.

"But your father will want you when he comes home." As she spoke she saw the tears in my eyes. She took my hand. "You are a blessing to us. I am happy you like it here." She and Uncle Samuel looked across the room at each other for several minutes, almost like they sent messages without having to speak.

Aunt Ivy said, "Niece, your grandmother is right. Your father cares for you. Besides, in another year you will have to attend high school. That means living in Sitka, among strangers."

She was right. Most kids who went to school in Sitka rarely ever got to come home. It would just be another kind of loneliness for me, and that's what I didn't want to go back to.

"You could ask your father if you might spend your summers here with us," Aunt Ivy said.

"Could I? You'd want me?" Her words made me fill up with joy.

Grandma Martha's eyes met mine and they smiled. "Yes," she said. "Ask him."

But what if he said no? What would I do? Had he read the last letter I sent him? Had it shown him how I felt? "What's the use of asking? I don't think he cares," I said.

"Whatever anger and sadness he has allowed to grow in him doesn't have to be yours," Grandma Martha said.

"It won't hurt for you to ask," Aunt Ivy said.

"Grandma Martha," I asked. "Do you think if I did live here, people would care that I'm only half Tlingit?"

"It is not what you were born with that matters," Grandma Martha said. "But how you build your life. That is how you will be judged."

Even with everything Grandma Martha and Aunt Ivy said, I was still afraid to ask my father. If he said no, would I ever see Tahkeen again?

Several days later, Aunt Ivy and I warmed up the troller and filled the tanks with fuel at the gas dock. Then we helped Uncle Samuel and Grandma Martha aboard. Uncle Samuel was to be examined by the doctor at the hospital. I knew they would be impressed with how much progress he had made. His ribs were still tender, but he breathed easily and had returned to carving. He exercised on his crutches every day, walking up and down the village street.

When the tanks were full, Aunt Ivy restarted the engine. The noise vibrated in our ears, and the sharp smell of diesel fuel surrounded the boat. Uncle Samuel smiled his approval at Aunt Ivy when she took the helm with confidence and steered the boat out of the bay.

"She runs the boat well, like a nephew," he said.

"Uncle Samuel!" she said.

But Uncle Samuel poked Grandma Martha to show he was making a joke. Aunt Ivy saw him and laughed. "You will be a good fisherman," he said. "And soon I will be your deckhand."

How warmly and gracefully Uncle Samuel lives his life, I thought. Even when, against his will, he must give up his boat and job, he does it with love.

"I am looking forward to it, Uncle," Aunt Ivy said

gently. "And when school is finished for the year, Clearie can fish with me. Won't we be the talk of the fleet?"

"It will be such a shock for all those salty old fishermen to see us running a boat that they'll forget to let out their lines, and we'll get all the salmon," I said.

The sea was calm for the whole trip to Sitka. When the sun set it looked huge. The air around it shimmered as if the ball of fire actually sank into the ocean, causing the water to boil and steam. Soon after, the stars came out and it got cold.

"If we were going to be out all night, we would see the northern lights," Uncle Samuel said.

"There's the Little Dipper," I said.

"I heard an elder say once that the Dipper stars held a person's life inside and let it out one drop at a time," Grandma Martha said. "And when it becomes empty it is the person's time to die."

"It looks empty to me," I said.

"No, Granddaughter. For you, it is full," Grandma Martha said.

Not if I were to leave here and never come back, I thought to myself.

The next day, Uncle Samuel's visit to the doctor was short. Soon we were on our way back to Tahkeen. We picked up Mark and gave him a ride home from school for the weekend. When I was at the wheel concentrating on the water ahead, I suddenly felt someone watching me. I looked behind me where Mark was sitting with Uncle Samuel. I strained to hear their conversation over the engine sound. Mark was listening with an amused looked on his face to what Uncle Samuel was saying.

"She and Ivy rebuilt it," Uncle Samuel said. "Little Clearie now has the arms of a man."

Mark laughed. "She still looks like a girl to me."

Hearing their words, I blushed and felt clumsy. My mind must have wandered away from driving the boat because Aunt Ivy said, "Hey, Niece, you wish to go back to Sitka?"

I started at the sound of her voice and looked out over the wheel. While thinking about Mark I had steered the boat in a wide arc and was going completely in the wrong direction. In my embarrassment I spun the wheel quickly the opposite way, sending items sliding on the deck and people catching their balance.

"Whoa there," they all said.

After that, we took the time to practice baiting the hooks on the metal fishing cables that were suspended from two long poles on the troller. When we were traveling or at anchor, the poles stayed in an upright position and hooked together overhead. When we fished, we lowered the poles so they stuck out from the boat, suspended over the water. The four lines with several baited hooks on each one were then released. We moved at the slowest possible speed the engine would run, dragging the lines so fish below could see the bait and go after it. Later we pulled in the lines and removed any fish caught, rebaited the hooks, and let them out again.

Uncle Samuel watched the whole process and announced, "You are ready to fish." Plus, we caught our dinner.

When we arrived back in Tahkeen, we took the boat into the gas dock and let Uncle Samuel and Grandma Martha off before anchoring in the bay. Tom Jonee was there outside his store rinsing a bucket with seawater. But as we approached he quickly turned away and went inside. We saw him pull down the brown window shade as if the store was closed.

"That's strange," Mark said. "Since Henry left, my father said Tom Jonee was being very polite and friendly."

"It is strange," I said. "He made a point of telling Grandma Martha that we were welcome in his store."

"We will know what is going on soon enough," Grandma Martha said. "Now Samuel must go home and rest."

Mark threw his duffel bag onto the dock and helped Uncle Samuel to step over the rail. "Here, let me walk with you."

It didn't take long for Aunt Ivy and me to moor the boat and paddle ashore. By the time we walked in the house several people were already there, including Irtha and Mary Ruth.

"What's going on?" I whispered to Mary Ruth inside the door. Grandma Martha and Irtha were sitting at the table. Irtha looked angry and Grandma Martha leaned close to her with a very worried expression. I noticed the teakettle hadn't even been put on.

"He is the devil. The cause of all my problems," Irtha said.

Mary Ruth whispered to me, "Henry Jonee is back."

17

Eulachon Moon

Saak Dis

For the next couple of weeks Henry Jonee kept out of sight. He didn't start running whiskey again and was never in the store. We all wondered why he had returned. He came up in conversation often. Knowing he was around was hard on Mary Ruth's mother. She told us, "He should go away and never come back."

"He probably is gone," Aunt Ivy said. "Nobody has seen him in weeks."

"But his skiff is still here," I said.

"There are other ways to leave Tahkeen," Aunt Ivy said. "Perhaps he rode out with a fisherman from Sitka. I think it is time to stop worrying about Henry Jonee."

I hoped Aunt Ivy was right.

Aunt Ivy now joined the procession of canoes each morning, crossing the water to the fishing boats. She plowed the troller down the bay, through fog and rain, out to the salmon fishing grounds. The work was hard. She came home exhausted and fell into bed, often without eating or even taking off her fish-splattered clothes.

"Ivy's fish will not leave," Grandma Martha said, carrying Aunt Ivy's bedding out to be scrubbed. "She sells their bodies to the cannery boat, but their spirits follow her home like old dogs."

There was no snow left even on the highest hills. It only rained and rained and rained.

"Grandma Martha," I said. "I bet I know what April is by the Tlingit calendar."

"What month, Granddaughter?"

"Month of Wet Like a Duck," I said, thinking of all the rain.

"No, no," she said. "It is *Saak Dis*, month of the eulachon's return."

"Not those fish you use to make that horrible stinky oil Uncle Samuel is always dipping his food in?"

"Yes. And it is delicious when you accustom yourself to it," she said.

Eulachon was a tiny fish, much like a sardine only with a stronger smell.

"Yuck, isn't smelling Aunt Ivy all the time bad enough?" I said. "Irtha said she put eulachon oil on her garden patch last summer. It stank all winter right up through the snow. I smelled it every time I walked by."

"Good stuff," Grandma Martha said, almost giggling.

True to the month's name, one morning at breakfast we heard Mary Ruth's brother, Douglas, yelling in the street. Uncle Samuel pulled himself up on his crutches and opened the door.

"Fish are running. Fish!" Douglas announced as he skipped by the houses.

Uncle Samuel's eyes lit up and he seemed to grow stronger and younger with the news. "Niece," he said. "Go tell the Fosters, no school today. Fish are coming."

Aunt Ivy and Grandma Martha began to move quickly, gathering items from the kitchen.

"I don't understand what's going on," I said.

"We will go to fish camp on the river," Aunt Ivy said. "The eulachon are starting to run."

"They return to the river to lay eggs?"

"Yes, they are the first. Chinook salmon will follow," Aunt Ivy said.

"Each year the eulachon bring the spring," Grandma Martha said. "They carry new life to the people after the long darkness."

I ran down to the school and, since it was early, knocked on the door. Mrs. Foster came and looked out. "Good morning, Clearie. Is everything all right?"

"Uncle Samuel sent me to tell you the eulachon are running."

"Oh, good news," she said. Then she yelled behind her, "Ernest, eulachon are running."

"Well, ring the bell," I heard Reverend Foster answer.

"Do you really cancel school?"

"Yes, of course," Mrs. Foster said. "The whole village goes to fish camp."

So we all went to fish camp. I helped Aunt Ivy load the canoe. We were to take the camp gear and equipment we would need to catch and cook, or render, the tiny fish into the smelly oil that people here loved. After we took the equipment to our spot on the river, one of us would return for Uncle Samuel and Grandma Martha.

While loading the canoe I saw that it was true; every household except the Jonees was doing the same thing we were. Even with James gone, there were Mary Ruth and Douglas along with their mother, carrying lanterns, fishnets, and buckets across the beach. Further down, line after line of people also got ready. I started to feel the excitement that seemed to be rushing through the whole village.

On the river, every family had its special place it went back to each year. Grandma Martha and Uncle Samuel had one of the best places, about four miles upstream on the shore directly across from Seigan Island.

Just like us, eagles followed the returning fish. I watched as more and more birds appeared, sitting in the cottonwood trees and sweeping down over the river to pick up eulachon.

"Eagle has a sweet voice," Grandma Martha said,

watching them. "And nice manners compared to old Raven. Raven will steal the fish right from my tub if I don't keep an eye on him."

Down next to the water was a metal oil barrel, cut in half the long way and set on cement blocks above a fire pit. This was where the fish were dumped after we scooped them out of the river with a pole net. The fire under the barrel was kept going all the time until the fish cooked down to what looked like slime. Then it was strained and the oil was put in covered buckets to keep over the winter.

Each dip of the net brought up a hundred or more of the flopping little fish. With the first scoops Grandma Martha laughed and clapped her hands. "Welcome, welcome," she said. Then she became more serious and set to work tending her fire so it would be just right for cooking the fish.

"In the old days," Aunt Ivy said as we piled wood for the fire, "the fish were dumped into a canoe that was half buried in the gravel and fish were rendered by dropping hot rocks into the hull. It took a long time."

Once the whole process got going, the week we spent at fish camp was a lot of fun. After a couple of days I even stopped noticing the smell. Between taking turns stirring the brew and tending the fire, there was time to go visiting, especially after we scooped out as many fish as we could use and were waiting for the last of them to process. On Sunday Reverend Foster held church service around the fire pit at their camp. Only Mark was missing; he stayed at school to study.

One afternoon I went to visit Mary Ruth across the river at their camp. The dry wind sounded like a whining dog as it brushed through the bare alders and last year's grass stalks.

I paddled over, but there wasn't a good place to beach my canoe so I went some ways downstream. After tying my boat to a tree limb, I struggled on the trail through the undergrowth. I almost ran right into Henry Jonee.

He was walking quickly toward the village with his head down and a rifle over his shoulder. I couldn't believe how filthy he looked. His clothes were torn and covered in mud. I could smell how dirty he was even after I took a scared step back.

First anger covered his face, then caution. He kept glancing over through the brush. I looked over, too. Irtha's camp was just on the other side of a large tree. I could plainly see Irtha stirring her vat of fish.

"What are you doing here?" I said loudly, hoping Irtha or Mary Ruth would hear me. I felt sweat on my forehead.

Henry looked back and forth between me and Irtha. "Uh," was all he said and stomped past me. But after a few steps he turned back and snarled, "Did your picture come out?"

"No," I awkwardly spit out a lie. "The wet ruined my camera."

With my answer he blended away into the trees and was gone. I didn't want him to know that the picture existed, even if it was worthless.

I rushed over to join Mary Ruth. Even though it was just a few steps I was panting when I got there.

"I just passed Henry Jonee on the trail," I said.

"Did he hurt you?" Irtha asked.

I was shaking so hard I could barely answer, "No, but he looked horrible," I said.

"I bet he's living out in the woods someplace," Mary Ruth said. "That's why we haven't seen him in Tahkeen."

"He is probably returning to burn our homes since he knows we are away," Irtha said.

On the last day of fish camp I took the canoe out and paddled the short distance to Seigan Island. It was the place Mark had taken me last fall, where he said the ancient Tlingits would go to see the future.

I knew I wouldn't run into Henry Jonee again because I could see the whole island from our camp. Aunt Ivy said she would keep an eye on me, too.

I landed the canoe on the shore. In the gray sky, several eagles circled directly above the pointed hilltop of the tiny island. As I walked across the beach I thought about what I hoped to see. Would I ever return to Tahkeen? Another month had passed and I was still afraid to write to my father and ask his permission to spend summers here.

I tried to imagine what he might say if I did ask him.

Would it anger him? Or would he be glad to be rid of me? Either way, I wasn't sure I wanted to know.

Climbing to the top of the hill I looked downriver. The south wind was strong, and it almost felt as if it held me up when I leaned into it. The smoke of all the campfires circled the island like wispy ribbons. On each hazy stream the smell of fish and water floated. I pictured the people who sat around the fire that was the source of each smoky line. At eight miles, the Hoskets; nine and a half miles, the Fosters; at Cottonwood Bend, Irtha, Mary Ruth, and Douglas; and where the grass sloped into the shallows, were Grandma Martha, Uncle Samuel, and Aunt Ivy.

I smelled every particle the wind carried. The fishy smoke flowed into my veins through my nose. I let my hopes peer into the future. And I started to see myself right in Grandma Martha's house, sitting beside Aunt Ivy weaving my own *naaxein*.

It was like the wind spoke to me, because suddenly, I knew for the first time that what Grandma Martha said was true. I could build my own tomorrow, exactly like the new pilothouse on the boat. If I wanted to belong in Tahkeen it didn't matter what my father or anybody thought — someday I would return. As soon as I could find some paper I would write my letter.

It was starting to rain, so I ran down the hill and climbed into the canoe, feeling like I had new bones to stand on and new eyes to see with.

18

War Dagger

Shal'ats

Late June came, and still I waited for an answer from my father. It had been almost two months since I wrote him asking to spend summers in Tahkeen.

School let out for the year, and I began to fish with Aunt Ivy. She also hired Reverend Foster. He liked to earn extra money for a vacation down south. Mark came home for the summer. But I hardly ever got to see him. Every day I fished with Aunt Ivy, and he was busy fishing on his father's boat.

One evening as Aunt Ivy, Reverend Foster, and I were coming into the bay after fishing we spotted a boat we didn't recognize at the dock.

"It's a big diesel job," Reverend Foster said. "Flying the territorial flag."

When we came closer we saw it was the sheriff's boat. We tied up at the gas dock, where two officers were speaking to Tom Jonee. Other people from the village were standing around in groups.

"My son is not here," Tom Jonee was saying to them.

After securing our lines, Reverend Foster walked up to the policemen. "What's going on?" he asked.

One of the officers greeted Reverend Foster, "I'm territorial Deputy Charlie Tonson. We are looking for a man named Henry Jonee. He's wanted for questioning concerning an arson fire on March tenth in Juneau."

That would have been during the time Henry was gone, I thought.

"Have any of you seen Mr. Jonee recently?" Deputy Tonson asked.

"I saw him in April," I said.

"Yes," the deputy said. "But his father said he has since left the village without saying where he was going."

Before thinking about what I was doing I said, "Henry Jonee also tried to burn my uncle's boat."

Deputy Tonson glanced over at the new yellow wood on the boat cabin.

"I took a picture of him doing it," I said. I saw Tom Jonee glare at me, and I suddenly wished I had spoken more quietly.

"You have a picture of this man?" Deputy Tonson asked.

"Yes, but you can't really tell he's on my uncle's boat," I said, feeling Tom Jonee still watching me.

"Does it show his face?"

"Yes," I said.

"I would like to see it if I could. It could help us with our investigation," he said.

"It's at my house," I said.

I looked over to where the other officer was still talking to Tom Jonee a few steps away. In a loud voice Tom Jonee said, "My son did not start any fire." Everyone heard him.

"Would you go get the picture for me?" the deputy asked.

I set off running as fast as I could. Five minutes later I came back and handed the photo to Deputy Tonson.

"Tell me," he said looking at the picture. "What is this that looks like a face right below Henry's leg?"

He held the photo out for me to see. There was an object that had what looked like two eyes, a nose, and a mouth on it.

"That's the handle of Uncle Samuel's fishnet," I said. "He carved a face into the wood."

"Well, I can't say for sure, but that may help prove Henry Jonee was on your uncle's troller."

"It could?" I was so excited that my picture might be good after all and Henry would be punished for what he did.

At that moment I saw Tom Jonee turn and walk away. The other officer hurried over and tapped Deputy Tonson on the shoulder while pointing to Tom Jonee leaving.

"Mr. Jonee," Charlie Tonson called. "I have a few more questions I need to ask you."

Tom Jonee looked around nervously. "I have supplies to unload," he said.

"Then we will come and speak with you as you work."

Everyone could feel Tom Jonee's fear. It darted around us like a fly in the air. Tom Jonee started to lead the policemen around to the back of the building.

As they left I caught a small movement at the store's window. A face appeared through the glass. Henry Jonee was hiding in the store where he could see and probably hear everything.

"Henry's there!" I yelled.

The two officers turned back. In the same second, the door of the store burst open and Henry Jonee came running out, his wild hair waving around his face. He carried a rifle and aimed it straight at me. "You!" he screamed.

I couldn't move. I couldn't breathe. I couldn't even move my eyes the slightest bit to find Aunt Ivy.

"I'll get you," Henry snarled, putting his finger on the trigger.

"Stop!" Deputy Tonson shouted.

Both he and the other officer pulled pistols from leather hip holsters. People scattered.

A huge pounding bang blew by me. I felt the wood dock near my feet splinter. The two policemen started after Henry as he ran off down the center of the village.

As soon as he began to move I felt every muscle in my body collapse. I fell on the ground screaming and crying with my hands over my face. Instantly, someone's arms came around me. "Clearie, are you hurt?" I heard Aunt Ivy ask. I threw my arms around her as hard as I could. "It's okay, I'm here. I'm here," she whispered.

I don't know how long Aunt Ivy held me but finally she said, "Mother and Uncle Samuel, they're alone in the house. We must go to them. Stay along the beach." She held my hand as we moved under the pilings. At our house we crawled up to the street and peered out from between the buildings.

"There they are," I said. My voice still shook so hard words scratched in my throat.

Deputy Tonson and the other man were kneeling behind a large tree stump pointing their guns toward the deserted house right next to the one Henry Jonee had burned. In the upstairs window I saw the top of Henry Jonee's head.

"I must tell them to stay inside," Aunt Ivy said about Grandma Martha and Uncle Samuel.

We crawled on our stomachs up to the wooden walkway, trying to stay out of sight.

"Henry Jonee," Deputy Tonson shouted. "Surrender. Throw the weapon out and come to where we can see you with your hands placed on top of your head."

When I heard the voice yelling, I stopped and covered my head in fear.

"Keep going," Aunt Ivy said. "We must get home."

I made myself continue. By this time the door was just a few feet in front of us. I glanced to the old house but didn't see Henry Jonee. Aunt Ivy reached for the door handle above us, white in her dark hand.

"Come out," Deputy Tonson shouted again. We scurried in and closed the door.

Once inside we both stood up. I looked around but didn't see Grandma Martha or Uncle Samuel.

"Mother? Uncle Samuel?" Aunt Ivy called. Then I saw them huddled together on Uncle Samuel's cot beside the cook stove that was tucked back in the far corner under the stairway.

A shot sounded from across the street. Aunt Ivy and I dropped down and slid through the dust on the floor to Grandma Martha and Uncle Samuel. The dirt rose around us and tasted like fear. When we reached them we put our arms around each other as if we could build a bulletproof shield to keep us safe.

The moments passed by slowly. Those sweater-covered arms around me, with the smell of wool and fish, were my anchor line. I saw shiny sweat on Uncle Samuel's face. Then I felt a drop of sweat in my hair, but my hands were cold. I thought, if any of us let go right now the others will drift away.

Finally, after the air stayed quiet for some time, Aunt Ivy stood up. As soon as she did I felt a cold draft against me from the hole she left in our circle.

"Do you think it's over?" Grandma Martha asked.

Aunt Ivy slowly walked across the room like she was crossing the river on spring ice. She hid between the door and the window that looked across to where Henry Jonee was holed up. Then she stretched her head in front of the glass.

"The police are walking to the house," she said. "I can't see Henry Jonee."

"Maybe he is shot," Grandma Martha said.

When she said that, I felt such a horrible mix of feelings. In a way, I wanted Henry to be dead. He was a monster that tried to shoot me.

"They are coming out," Aunt Ivy said. "First is Deputy Tonson, then Henry. The other policeman is behind him and Henry is handcuffed."

"Let us hope no one is hurt," Uncle Samuel said almost like a prayer.

We all went to look together.

"Henry looks like he's in pain," I said. "There's blood on his sleeve."

Henry walked between the policemen in defeat. The second officer held Henry's gun. When they passed we opened our door and stepped out to watch them return to the police boat.

All down the street others came out of their houses after the three men walked by. The doors opening and people moving was like the village taking a deep sigh of relief. We fell into walking behind, leaving a large distance between the three men and ourselves.

Once on the boat, Deputy Tonson bandaged Henry's arm and then put him, still handcuffed, inside the cabin. The other officer led Tom Jonee out of the store. He was in handcuffs, too.

I looked around at all the familiar faces. Many returned my glances with looks of concern for me. Aunt Ivy kept her arm around me the whole time. I was grateful for her support.

"Why do they arrest Tom Jonee as well?" Grandma Martha asked.

"He lied to the police," Aunt Ivy said. "And he hid Henry from them."

Then Deputy Tonson saw me and came over to where we stood watching.

"Are you all right, miss?" he asked.

I nodded.

"Henry Jonee will have a lot more to answer for than just the Juneau arson," he said. "You may have to testify in court."

"We understand," Aunt Ivy said.

The other officer started the engine, and we watched Deputy Tonson jump aboard.

Reverend Foster came over to us. "Were you hurt, Clearie?"

"I'm fine," I managed to say.

"I'm glad everyone is safe," Reverend Foster said. "I must take Mrs. Foster home. She is still very upset."

"Let's go home as well," Uncle Samuel said. Grandma Martha held his sleeve as they moved slowly in front of me.

Once we came through the door Grandma Martha turned to me and took a deep shaky breath. "I'll boil tea," she said. When she spoke those words to let us know everything would be fine, I ran to her and held her round neck in a tight hug. She was surprised and then she put her arms around me and rocked me gently. "We are all together. We are all safe at home," she said.

19

An Eagle's Foot

Ch'aak' du x'oos

The next morning none of us knew quite what to do. We sat at the breakfast table long after the food was gone. Grandma Martha looked at me, I looked at Uncle Samuel, and Aunt Ivy stared out the window. It was almost like the showdown with Henry Jonee stopped time, and we were waiting for something to start it again. Or maybe it was just the usual summer rain that seemed to keep us trapped inside.

Finally Aunt Ivy stood up and started to put on her green rain gear. "I have a boat to clean," she said. She looked at me as if waiting for me to follow. For some reason I wanted to stay home. Uncle Samuel said, "It is time for me to get back to work. This cast itches where I can't reach. Work will help me forget."

"Come then," Aunt Ivy said. She stopped after she said it and laughed nervously. "I'm sorry, Uncle. I sounded like I was issuing orders."

"As you should, Captain Ivy," Uncle Samuel answered smiling.

"Are you ready, Clearie?" Aunt Ivy asked.

"Can I stay home today? I'd like to visit Mary Ruth if I could."

"She has earned a rest," Grandma Martha said.

"Yes," Aunt Ivy agreed. "You should see your friends and catch up after all that has happened. But in a few days we must be ready to fish again."

When I left the house I saw that people were gathering down by the store. Mary Ruth was among them, so I went to see her there. Everyone was discussing what would happen now that both Jonees had been arrested.

"My mother asked me to go to the store for her yesterday morning," Mary Ruth said. "I didn't do it, and now there is no store."

I stood near Mary Ruth. "There's a store, just no one to run it."

Reverend and Mrs. Foster joined the group. Mrs. Foster gave me a hug. "I'm so thankful you're safe."

Reverend Foster said, "I don't know exactly what the police will charge Tom Jonee with. He could be gone for some time."

"I don't think he will come back," Mrs. Foster said. "He should be ashamed to face us."

Others agreed. "We need supplies now. Some things can't wait," Mr. Simons added.

"I need canned milk and tea," Mary Ruth told me. "I was going to make a milk custard."

"Well," said Mr. Hosket. "I say we open it up and take turns sitting behind the counter. We'll just leave the money in a box until we know what should be done."

No one moved. It almost felt like walking into someone's house when they weren't there.

"Who's to be the first storekeeper?" Mr. Hosket called out trying to make light of people's discomfort.

"Let's have the Reverend do it," Mr. Simons said. "It seems more honest having him."

"Okay, either Mrs. Foster or myself will sit for an hour every morning. How would that be?" Reverend Foster said. Then he turned to Charlie Hosket. "Maybe Mark could help out with the heavy work."

It was agreed. Reverend Foster pushed opened the unlocked door and announced, "Tahkeen General is now open for business." We all followed them inside.

After Mary Ruth bought her milk we decided to walk together down the beach. The stones were slippery, but the rain made their colors and patterns stand out clearly. We stopped and picked up several pretty ones.

"We're leaving next week to work in the cannery at Elbott Bay," Mary Ruth said. "All of us, Mother, Douglas, and me."

"I know, Grandma Martha told me."

"We won't have any money to live on if we don't. Mother heard that Father is in Sitka, but he doesn't send us anything."

I tried to think of something encouraging to say. "You're lucky you have your mother."

"Do you miss yours?"

"Not so much since I came to Grandma Martha's." We walked on a little further. "When will you be back from Elbott Bay?"

"I don't know. We may not come back. There's no work here."

I thought again about the village someday becoming deserted. It made everything I had learned since coming to Tahkeen so much more important. "We must write to each other, no matter where you go or I go. Promise?" I said.

"I promise," Mary Ruth said. We hugged, and as we did the brims of our rain hats bent and the water ran down my neck. "That's cold," I yelled, and jumped back. We ended not with crying but with laughing.

"I must go," Mary Ruth said. "Milk custard takes time to make." She ran toward the village.

I walked back more slowly. The summer ahead seemed misty like the clouds and wood smoke mingling over the roofs of the houses. When I reached the dock I sat with my legs dangling over the edge and my long raincoat tucked under me. I could see Aunt Ivy lean over the side of the boat out in the bay. She scooped up a bucket of water and poured it on the deck to scrub off dried fish scales and dirt. She disappeared from view when she knelt down.

I sat and watched the waves for a long time until I felt a hand on my shoulder. I stood up and turned around. Mark stepped so close to me that I smelled the wet flannel and wood smoke scent of his shirt and felt his warm breath cross my forehead.

"I thought about you last night when the police were after Henry. If you hadn't spoken up, Henry would have stayed hidden," he said.

"Really?"

"I thought you were very brave. Oh yes." He reached into his raincoat pocket and pulled out a thin envelope. "This letter was at the store for you, from your father." Rain dripped off his hair over his eyes. He squinched his brows to keep the water out and still tip his head down to look at me.

I opened the letter and read it silently, all the time feeling Mark watch me. I smiled and then hugged the letter tight against me.

"You have good news?" he asked.

"Yes, listen," I said.

Dear Clearie,

I am holding the last two letters you sent me and I have read them over so many times. I realize they are from a daughter I have never known, or perhaps just couldn't see,

I don't know. I do know you have found a place where you're happy and I'm glad. I want you to spend summers with your grandmother if that's what you choose. But she is right, you must go to school down here where you can live at home. I just hope that you will give me another chance to be with the Clearie who has written these letters and seems to be growing up into such an interesting young woman. After your mother left I was empty for the longest time. I felt I was a failure to her. But I know now that it was us I should have been trying to help.

Your father

"That's wonderful," he said in a shout. He grabbed me around the waist in a hug and swung me in a circle.

I put my arms around him and held on. Under my fingers I could feel every fish hauled over the side of a boat and every load of wood carried, worn into his muscles.

As he put me down I looked up at him. Just then, an eagle passed over our heads so close I could almost feel its shadow breeze across my head. Its hard-gold eye stared into mine. I could see the bird's yellow talons folded in on themselves under a fan of white tail feathers.

"I'll be in Tahkeen every summer, every moment I can," I said. "Even if I have to catch a ride hanging on to an eagle's foot and fly."

As we stood there, the wind from the south gusted up

and blew so strong it almost knocked us off our feet. Our arms dropped and we looked down the bay. Clouds were rolling across the surface of the water, and the waves were becoming big and forceful.

Below the house, Aunt Ivy beached the canoe. Uncle Samuel secured it to the winch on the piling. He then carefully began to make his way up to the house on his crutches.

"It's getting stormy," Mark said. "That eagle was smart to head for the trees."

"I want to go tell them about my letter," I said.

Back at the house I didn't say anything while Aunt Ivy and I carried load after load of tools and rope up to the house from the canoe. With each trip Aunt Ivy worried. "This storm came so sudden. I hope the anchor line is secure. Did you get the metal bucket or did I leave that on the boat? Did you double-check the canoe line?"

On the last trip into the house Uncle Samuel said, "Niece, you fret like the waves. Sit. Stop. There is no more work to do today."

We changed into dry clothes, and Grandma Martha stoked the stove. She set pans of bread into the oven to bake.

Then, without a word, I stood in the middle of the room and held the letter above my head. Everyone saw it and became quiet.

At last Aunt Ivy said, "Well?"

"He said yes!" I yelled. We all started hugging and laughing until we had to sit and wipe our eyes.

"Does Mark know?" Uncle Samuel asked with a wink.

My cheeks were suddenly hot. "He gave me the letter."

We sat at the table until Grandma Martha jumped up. "My bread!" And we all fell back into everyday motions.

The wind and rain wrapped itself like a blanket around the little house. I could feel it sway on its pilings. But it was a gentle rocking, a feeling of comfort that held us tight.

Aunt Ivy sat down in front of her loom, her body lowered onto her crossed legs like a sigh. I sat down at my empty loom next to her.

"It is so seldom I can do this anymore," she said. Her fingers ran across the wool. "I sometimes hear the yarn calling to me. That sounds strange doesn't it?"

"No, it doesn't," I said. "It calls to me, too. Will you teach me now?"

I picked up the yarn and followed Aunt Ivy as she fell into motion. Across the room, Uncle Samuel began carving on a small piece of wood, and Grandma Martha moved back and forth between the stove and the sink.

This is how things should always be I thought: house, wool, family, forever.

From behind me, Grandma Martha said, "I'll boil tea."

Roman temple Maison Carree in the city of Nimes

The Arena, Arles, Provence, France